Laurell [...] or of the
acclaim[...]. She lives
near St [...] two dogs
and an ever-fluc[...]nvites you to
vis[...] her website at www.laurellkhamilton.org.

[...]views for the Anita Blake, Vampire Hunter, Novels

'[...]at *The Da Vinci Code* did for the religious thriller, the
A[...]ta Blake series has done for the vampire novel'
USA Today

'Wildly popular'   *Entertainment Weekly*

'Hamilton's complex, enthralling world is utterly absorbing'
Booklist

'A hardcore guilty pleasure'   *The Times*

'Laurell K. Hamilton is the reigning queen of the urban
fantasy world'   *Midwest Book Review*

'Alw[...]ys very, very sexy and exciting'   *Dreamwatch*

'Th[...] fast-paced, tough-edged supernatural thriller is mesmer-
izin[...] reading indeed'   *Locus*

'[...]ne action never stops'
The New York Review of Science Fiction

'Supernatural bad guys beware, night-prowling Anita Blake
is savvy, sassy and tough'   P N Elrod

I was enthralled by a departure from the usual type of
vampire tale. . .'   Andre Norton

'A real rush. . . a heady mix of romance and horror'
Jayne Ann Krentz

Anita Blake, Vampire Hunter, Novels

eSpecials

LAURELL K. HAMILTON

An Anita Blake,
Vampire Hunter, Novella

headline

First published in the United States of America in 2014
by the Penguin Random House Company
A Jove Book / published by arrangement with the author
Jove Books are published by The Berkley Publishing Group
JOVE® is a registered trademark of Penguin Group (USA) LLC.

First published in Great Britain in 2014
by HEADLINE PUBLISHING GROUP

1

Cataloguing in Publication Data is available from the British Library

ISBN 978 1 4722 2698 3

Typeset in Sabon Ltd Std

Printed and bound in Great Britain by Clays Ltd, St Ives plc

HEADLINE PUBLISHING GROUP
An Hachette UK Company
338 Euston Road
London NW1 3BH

www.headline.co.uk
www.hachette.co.uk

To my husband, Jon,
because in some ways everything is for him.
To Genevieve and her Spike,
figuring it out as we go.

We must be willing to get rid of the life we've planned, so as to have the life that is waiting for us. The old skin has to be shed before the new one can come.

Joseph Campbell

1

JASON SCHUYLER, ONE of my best friends and favorite werewolves, stood in the morning sunlight of the kitchen. His yellow hair gleamed in the light, so that his boyishly handsome face was haloed with sunshine, but as I looked into the pure, soft blue of his eyes I knew that devil's horns were more his style than halos, and pure was only a way to describe his eyes, not him. He'd been a precocious teenager and his day job was still assistant manager and exotic dancer at Guilty Pleasures. The body that showed around his tank top and jogging shorts proved that

1

he stayed in shape for his job, but none of that was what made halos seem wrong for him. He had a streak of mischief in him so strong that he couldn't quite resist pushing . . . everything. If the situation was tense he had to resist not making a wisecrack at the wrong moment; since I had the same urge, it was one of our bonding moments. He and I both tended to poke the proverbial badger with a stick until it rushed out of the hole and tried to eat us. We'd both learned over the years to curb this urge, and were much happier for controlling that part of us, but Jason still had that edge of deviltry to the smile on his face, and the shine in those spring-sky eyes.

I pushed my own thick black curls away from my face; they fell right back against my cheek, but sometimes it's the effort that counts. I sat at the kitchen table in my long silk robe, sipping coffee and watching that smile on his face. Either he was enjoying the hell out of getting us all out of bed at this outrageously early hour, or he was hiding behind the smile. Most of us have our blank face, a version of the cop face, and Jason hid behind a grin usually, but since he also spent a lot of time actually smiling, laughing, or grinning, it was great camouflage for whatever else he was thinking.

I tucked my robe a little closer across my chest, not because Jason hadn't seen me nude in the past, but because he'd asked for a conversation as his friend, not a friends-with-benefits booty call, so flashing breasts seemed inappropriate. It was tricky sleeping with someone who was actually your friend but never quite your boyfriend, a thin line to walk between true friendship and *hey, baby*.

"We all work nights, Jason; what was so important that you got us up this early?"

His grin widened, and he stepped forward enough that I could see his straight blond hair without the sunshine special effects. He'd cut his hair again, almost businessman short. He was one of the few men I knew who really did look better in shorter hair; it seemed to open up his face and make you see that he was handsome in his own right, when he wasn't clowning around or being irritating, though honestly that last part had almost gone away. I'd met Jason when he was nineteen; now at twenty-five he had grown up. I was only five or six years older than he was—depending on the time of year, our birthdays made us seem to gain or lose a year on each other. At twenty-five and thirty it wasn't a big age difference; at nineteen and twenty-five it had seemed like more.

"Let's wait for everyone else," he said, and sipped his own coffee. He didn't really drink a lot of coffee; he sipped at it, and would eventually put it down about half drunk and cold. Since we ground our own beans and used a French press to make the coffee, it was a waste of good, hot caffeine.

I huddled around my third cup of it, determined to make up for Jason's lack of enthusiasm.

Envy walked into the kitchen. She was five-eleven, so she towered over Jason and me. I was five-three and he was five-four. She'd combed her thick, almost shoulder-length blond hair, but hadn't bothered with makeup any more than I had. The strong cheekbones of her face seemed unfinished without the makeup, so that you got a glimpse of what she might have looked like at fifteen instead of the very grown-up early twenty-something. She'd thrown an oversized man's T-shirt over her, and on me it would have hung to midthigh, or even my knees; on her it barely covered her ass, so that she was all long golden legs as she padded barefoot into the room.

She was everything I'd wanted to be when I was a little girl: tall, blond, and Nordic-looking like my father and stepmother, and stepsister, and half brother, and . . . But I'd made peace with my mother's Mexican heritage that had given me black curls and dark brown eyes, and could even acknowledge that my skin was paler than Envy's and she tanned better than I did, which just seemed wrong. She blinked pale blue tiger eyes into the sunlight as if she were startled. None of us were morning people. The tiger eyes were literal; she was part of the golden tiger clan, which was one of the few inherited types of lycanthropy, and one of the ways they proved their pure bloodlines was that they were born with permanent tiger eyes in their human faces. Most of the other wereanimals I'd seen with animal eyes in human form had them because they'd spent too much time in their beast form. You could get stuck, and usually the eyes were the first thing to stick.

"Coffee's hot," I said.

"Tea," she muttered.

I started to tell her to help herself, and then realized she didn't know where the tea was, or anything. It was the first time Envy had stayed overnight at the house in Jefferson County. She lived at the Circus of the Damned with the bulk of our people, but she'd been dropped off here after her date with Richard Zeeman, wolf king, Ulfric of the local werewolves, and college biology professor. He had a house out here in Jefferson County, too, so it had made more sense for him to drop her here than driving her all the way back into the city to the Circus, but I wasn't sure I wanted them to make a habit out of it. Richard was sort of my ex; we'd even been briefly engaged. We still had sex occasionally, so having his current lover dropped at my house for a sleepover was a little weird. He'd offered to sleep over with Envy here, but I, and she, had vetoed it. We were all polyamorous, which means to love more, so everyone knew what and who everyone else was doing, but that didn't mean there weren't moments when too much sharing was, well, too much. Richard's work schedule was almost the opposite of mine, which meant that though we were lovers, it wasn't that frequent. Sex with him was great, but we'd both done a lot of emotional damage to each other over the years, and . . . the needs he'd met in my life were now met by other people, who liked, or loved, each other and got along a hell of a lot better with the other men. Richard was trying, but in some ways he'd worked out his shit too late to truly be a part of our happy little poly group. He sort of floated on the edges of my life, and I on his.

Envy had slept in one of the guest rooms, but still it was the first time she'd curled those long legs underneath my kitchen table.

Was I supposed to wait on her? Fetch her tea? I felt the first bubbling of anger, which was still one of my best things, when I didn't know what else to do.

"What kind of tea do you want?" Jason asked. He put his coffee down and went to the cabinets.

He'd stayed over enough to make tea without having to ask directions.

"Mint," she said, and laid her head on her arms so that she looked like she was going to take a nap on the table.

"Peppermint, spearmint, or a medley?" he asked.

"You pick," she muttered, not raising her head.

"Rough night?" I asked, sipping more of the strong black coffee.

She moved her head enough to roll an eye at me through the fall of yellow hair. It reminded me disturbingly of Dev, her cousin, who was also a weretiger of the gold clan, and one of my lovers. Dev was short for Devil, which was a nickname for Mephistopheles. Envy had gotten one of the better family names.

"You really need to have sex with him more often."

"You mean Richard?" I asked, because she was also sleeping with Jean-Claude, head vampire of the United States and my fiancé. I did mention that we were polyamorous, right? It wasn't cheating, because everyone got everyone else's permission, but it was complicated, sometimes very complicated.

"Yes," she said, still just looking at me with that one inhuman eye.

"Did Richard ask you to talk to me?"

"No," she said, and just looked at me as if waiting for me to say something. Was I supposed to pry information out of her?

"What made it a rough night?" Jason asked. He'd filled the rapid-heat electric kettle, and it was starting to warm up. He had a mug, and a tea bag was trailing out of it, waiting. There was actually loose-leaf tea in there somewhere, but no mint outside bags.

Envy turned her head enough to look at him, so that all I could see was the thick hair. "I don't think you'll understand."

"Try me, I'm very sympathetic." He grinned when he said it, which left a debate on whether he was really sympathetic or just kidding.

"He really is a good listener," I said.

She rolled her head back to look at me, and I realized that her hiding her face in her hair might be a stress reaction. What the heck had happened last night?

9

"He says you and he just can't get your schedules to match up for sex lately, is that true?" she asked.

"Yeah," I said, and drank more coffee; maybe if I just drank enough of it, I could do this conversation without losing my temper.

"Do you enjoy the sex?"

I drank more coffee. Maybe if I drowned myself in it? "Yes."

"When he's really rough in bed, how do you get him to stop?"

"You get him to stop by saying 'No, stop,' " I said.

She rose up enough to shake her head. "No? I can say no and he'll respect that? I mean, how do you tell him it's too rough?"

I fought not to frown at her. "I say, 'Ow, that hurt, stop it.' "

Jason piped up, "Or my favorite, 'Do that again and I'll kill you.' "

"You're not saying it right, Jason; it's 'Do that again and I will fucking kill you.' "

He laughed. "Oh, yeah, I forgot that part." He leaned against the cabinets, grinning at both of us.

I didn't feel like smiling, so I glared at him. His grin widened, eyes sparkling with it.

I shook my head and went back to huddling over my coffee. Jason was incorrigible; trying to corrige him just irritated me and amused the hell out of him.

"*Ow* really is a safeword for me," I said.

"Richard says you like rough sex—was he lying?"

I stared into my coffee, debating on whether to get up and add to the cup, or if I had the courage to look her in the face while we had this conversation. Fuck, courage it was.

I turned to look into those beautiful otherworldly eyes and said, "I like rough sex. I like sex with Richard. Now, what's up? What do you want to know, or say?"

She sat up straighter, squaring her shoulders. "Well, that is direct."

"I'm pretty sure I've had this conversation with other girlfriends of his over the years, so just say it, Envy. Did the sex get too rough last night?"

"Yes."

"And what do you want me to do about it?"

"Do you really like sex as rough as he does?"

I shrugged. "Yes, sometimes, not every night, but yeah."

She shivered. "Fine, Anita, you want to be direct, I can be direct. I had to tell him to stop, or ease up, constantly last night. He'd been great, the sex would be wonderful, he'd bring me to orgasm and then he'd start being too rough again, as if once he made me come he thought it earned him the right to be too rough and hurt me."

"Most women can take rougher intercourse after enough foreplay," Jason said. "He wasn't trying to be mean, just thought he'd done enough prep work to have sex the way he wanted to have it, and you'd enjoy it, too."

"Well, I didn't, and I had to keep telling him to stop. I finally told him to get off me, that was it."

"Do you mean for last night, or do you mean done as in done forever?" I asked.

She looked at me, and her eyes darkened the way that human eyes do when they start to get angry. "Forever. The sex is amazing if he can control himself, but he's so big that if he just starts pounding it hurts, and it drowns out all the orgasms, or even stops me from orgasming, because it hurts too much."

"I'm sorry he hurt you," I said. What else could I say?

"How long has it been since you've slept with him?"

"A while," I said.

"You can't remember?"

I shrugged again. "He's not one of my main sweeties. I . . . Maybe six weeks? He's trying to date some human woman, and it takes time to really date someone. Our booty calls had to take a backseat to him date-dating someone."

"As opposed to just fucking them," she said, and she sounded angry again.

"Yeah, dating takes more time than just fucking," I said. I fought not to get angry, or be offended, not to add any more emotion to what promised to be an emotional minefield.

"I enjoy sleeping with Jean-Claude, he's wonderful, but Richard is a brute in bed."

I so wanted out of this conversation, but it was like a train wreck—you knew it was coming, but sometimes you're still along for the ride.

"He can be, I guess."

Jason came to stand beside me, touched my shoulder. "Say the rest, Anita."

I looked up at him. "What rest?"

He looked at me, and it was that *you know* look. There weren't many people I'd take that look from, but Jason was on that short list.

"I like that he's rough. Sometimes a brute in bed is exactly what I want," I said.

She shuddered. "You can have him, I'm done."

"I don't want him as a boyfriend either, but the occasional sex is great, that was always fabulous between us."

"You look delicate, like he'd break you."

"Looks can be deceiving," I said.

Jason squeezed my shoulder. "The fact that Anita likes rough sex is one of the reasons I wanted everyone to meet this morning."

14

The comment made me look up at him. "What does that mean?"

The tea timer went off and he went to rescue it, and also neatly avoided answering my question.

I called after him. "What do my sexual preferences have to do with anything?"

"I'm getting the tea," he said with his back to us as he fished the bag out of the mug.

"What is this little meeting about this morning?" I asked, suspicious now.

Nathaniel spoke as he came into the kitchen. "It's about helping everybody in our poly group feel better."

He'd pulled on a pair of his favorite jeans, the ones that were nearly white with washing and had begun to thread out across the thighs. His knees peeked out of actual holes as he padded barefoot toward me. His ankle-length hair was in its usual braid so that it was mostly hidden behind him with only glimpses of the thick auburn rope peeking from behind him as he moved.

My smile of greeting changed to something less happy. "What does that mean, and why do I feel like you and Jason have been plotting behind my back about something?"

He smiled, and it was the real deal, not the one that he flashed at Guilty Pleasures to get customers to shove hundred-dollar bills down his pants. If they could have seen this smile full of love and lust and just . . . Nathaniel, they'd have found thousand-dollar bills to offer him in hopes that he'd deliver on everything that smile hinted at.

I fought to stay grumpy at him, but found it impossible as he crossed the golden bars of sunlight, turning his lavender eyes almost blue, as if they were paling in the warmth of all that sunshine. His eyes were truly the color of spring lilacs. Only two things made them darken to a truer purple: anger and lust. It had to be enough of both, and anger was a rarer cause for it than lust.

He changed his walk slightly so that I was suddenly aware of just how well he moved, how muscular and yummy his naked upper body was. He'd actually had to tone down his weight lifting because he was bulking up too much for the flexibility he needed as a dancer. He was learning, and starting to perform, some modern dance pieces, but it was the exotic dancer part of him that glided and strutted his way over to give me another good-morning kiss. We'd done more than kiss before I got out of bed to meet Jason in the kitchen.

He bent that handsome face over me where I sat, coming in for a kiss. "You know just how much you affect me, don't you?" I whispered.

"It's my job to know," he whispered back, and kissed me.

I kissed him back, because what else could I do? Hell, what else did I want to do? I wasn't angry enough not to run my hand around his bare waist and caress him as our lips met.

He rose and I smiled up at him, damn near stupid-faced with the kiss, and the memory of earlier, and all the days before. We'd been living together for three years and it just got better.

"That," Envy said, "that's what I want. I want

someone to look at me the way you two look at each other, or the way that Jason and J.J. look at each other. I want gentleness and love."

"Doesn't everybody?" Jason said, as he carried her tea to the table.

"No. Anita says she likes Richard being a brute, but she has Nathaniel, and Micah, and Jean-Claude. She has her gentle, and her love."

"You have Jean-Claude," I said.

"No, I have sex with Jean-Claude, I'm his lover, but he doesn't love me."

Nathaniel turned to her, one hand still in mine. "Are you in love with him?"

I stiffened, my hand tensing in his. "Nathaniel!"

"No, Anita, we need to know how we all really feel about each other. If we're not honest it all falls apart."

"He's right," Jason said. He sat down at the table at the end so he could see all of us easily.

I glared at him.

"Don't give me that look," he said, laughing. "You know it's true."

I tried to keep frowning at him, but started smiling

in spite of myself. Jason had had that effect on me from almost the beginning when I met him. It was one of the reasons that we were friends and that I hadn't killed him when I first met him; so glad I hadn't.

I finally gave in to the smile, but did my best to smother it in my coffee cup, though since I was still holding hands with Nathaniel, the tough-as-nails attitude was a little compromised.

Nathaniel pressed the back of my hand against his bare stomach and I suddenly had more trouble thinking. I looked up at him. "You're doing that on purpose, aren't you?"

"Doing what?" he asked, violet eyes wide. If it had been Jason I'd have known he was being disingenuous, but with Nathaniel just liked touching so much sometimes he did it without thinking.

"Nothing," I said.

Jason grinned at me from the other end of the table. I started to try to glare at him again, but finally said, "Fuck it, what's wrong, or what's up?"

Nathaniel raised my hand up so he could kiss it, and rub his cheek against it, like a cat scent-marking—*mine*. I liked it, because we were each other's *mine*; the fact that the word didn't include an exclusivity clause didn't make the possessive *mine* any less real, a point I just couldn't seem to explain to my monogamous friends.

"I'll get breakfast started while we wait for Domino. He's still in the shower."

Domino was one of our bodyguards, and one of my lovers, but he didn't sleep at this house much either. We were still organizing our guard rotation since we lost Ares, and I had been willing to believe that Domino was going to be more at the house because of that, but realizing he was going to be in on the talk this morning let me know it hadn't been a coincidence that the weretiger had slept over and shared a bed with Nathaniel and me. Our third, Micah Callahan, was traveling on business again, so the big bed had room for a guest.

"Tigers like water, a lot," I said, and sipped at my coffee.

"I'm not overly fond of it," Envy said, "but that

may be because you can never take a shower without a man thinking you want sex."

Nathaniel moved toward the oven, laughing softly. Jason started to laugh, too. I coughed and nearly aspirated coffee.

She gave me the full weight of those exotic blue eyes. "It must be true for you, too. Richard loves shower sex."

Jason laughed harder.

"What's so funny?" Envy asked, looking from one to the other of us.

Jason looked at me with sparkling eyes. This time I managed to glare at him, while I blushed. I'd almost stopped doing that—almost.

"Anita likes water," he said in a voice that was shiny with laughter.

"The new oven preheated just like it was supposed to," Nathaniel said, either because it was what interested him or to prove he wasn't poking this particular badger with a stick. He moved to the fridge to get the cinnamon rolls he'd made last night.

"Yeah, I like sex in water, but see if I climb into the shower with you anytime soon, laughing boy."

Jason quieted his laughter, and seemed trapped between looking pleased with himself and trying to pretend-pout at me.

"You and Richard seem perfect sexually for each other; why isn't he one of your main lovers?" Envy asked.

"Because outside the sex we had a lot of issues, and not all of them went away just because he's doing his therapy," I said, my voice a little hoarse from swallowing the coffee wrong. *Awkward* was putting it mildly.

"I'd wait to put in the cinnamon rolls, or else everybody will be down to have some once they fill the whole house with that great smell," Jason said.

Nathaniel looked up from the tray in his hand, nodded, and put it back in the fridge. Jason was right, but the fact that he'd said it out loud in time to keep that delectable scent from waking the rest of the household was the other reason he was my friend; he was smart and practical when he wanted to be, big emphasis on the *wanted to be*.

Nathaniel came to sit beside me, on the other side from Envy. I put my hand under the table so I could play along the threads and bare skin peeking through his jeans; they were one of my favorite pairs of jeans on him, too.

"Anita's being nice, but the truth is that Richard doesn't like me, and I don't like him," Nathaniel said.

"I've noticed he seems sort of conflicted about you. It's like he's trying to be fair, but he has trouble where you're concerned; why is that?"

I slid my fingers through the threads of his jeans so I could touch more of his bare skin. "You want to explain it?" he asked, putting his hand over mine to stop me from caressing quite that much, and the fact that he'd stopped me from petting him and was trying to force me to talk about Richard was as big a clue as any of how much he didn't like him.

I sighed and said, "Richard is a big, handsome, athletic guy, and even the best of them are used to winning."

"You mean with women?" she asked.

"That, and physical stuff. He's used to being able

to date pretty much any woman he wants, and if he gets out of his own way in a fight, he can hold his own against most nonprofessional fighters."

"So?" she said.

"So," Jason said, "he's used to winning."

She looked at all of us, frowning. "I don't understand what that has to do with him and Nathaniel not getting along."

"I won," Nathaniel said.

"Won what?"

"Anita, being permanently in her life, being her main squeeze, her person, hers, and she's mine. Micah and I have what Richard wants."

"You mean Anita."

He shrugged, and half-nodded. "Anita, and a life that works, and makes us all happy."

"He's sleeping with Anita, and he could still have a life with someone else."

"He could, but no one is Anita."

That made me uncomfortable, and I fought not to squirm. "It's not like that."

"I think Richard could have shared you with

24

Jean-Claude, because he sees him as dominant, big enough, beautiful, another guy who's used to winning, so they could have shared," Jason said.

"But other than the beautiful part, I'm none of those things," Nathaniel said, "and Richard can't get past that someone like me won."

"I'm not a prize to be won, damn it," I said.

"I know that, and that's one of the reasons I'm here, and Richard isn't."

I met Nathaniel's so-serious gaze and realized there was more truth there than I wanted to admit. "We're making Richard sound arrogant, and he's not."

"Why do you feel you have to defend him?" Nathaniel asked.

"I don't know, maybe because I was in love with him once, or maybe because he's still my lover and I feel guilty about that."

"Why guilty?" Envy asked.

"I'm not sure, but there's some guilt tied up with him."

"I was there, Anita; he blew his chance to be with you over and over," Jason said, "and he doesn't like me for a lot of the same reasons he doesn't like Nathaniel and Micah."

"We're just friends with benefits," I said.

Jason nodded, and sipped his coffee.

"Richard is your wolf king; is he making your life hard in the pack?"

Jason looked down.

"Talk to me," I said.

"I'll never be high in the pack hierarchy, Anita, but that's because I'm more a lover than a fighter." He grinned, trying to make a joke of it.

"Is Richard taking his feelings out on you?"

"Not really. I can fight enough to hold my own and not be picked on in the pack, but I'll never be good enough to rise much, and honestly I don't want to be in charge."

"I know you're more dominant than you let on, but that you truly don't want to be in charge of the other werewolves," I said.

"Not even a little bit," he said, and took another sip of coffee.

"So, you're all saying that Richard sees Nathaniel,

Micah, and even Jason as not worthy to have won the fair maiden," Envy said.

"Something like that," I said.

"I don't think it's in the front of his head," Nathaniel said, and squeezed my hand.

"How he feels about Nathaniel and me is," Jason said. "We are literally further down in the structure of our animal groups, and he's the Ulfric, the leader. Among the wolves, that means that anything he wants is pretty much his, and he knows that he could kick our asses, but here we sit, happier and more a part of Anita's life than he is, and that is what he has trouble accepting."

"But Micah is Nimir-Raj, leopard king, and the head of the Coalition, so he's becoming like the leader for all the animal groups in town, and even across the country. Why does Richard have an issue with him?"

"Because Micah is five-three and Richard is six-one," Jason said.

"What?" Envy asked.

"You know how most women walk into a room

and assess the beauty in the room to see where they rate, and who might give them a run for their money?" Jason asked.

"Sure," Envy said.

"A lot of men do the same thing, but they're not looking at who's better-looking, they're assessing threats, physical potential."

Envy gave him wide eyes.

"No, really, they do," I said.

"I don't," Nathaniel said.

"Me, either, but that's because we both know that we are not the biggest, baddest man in the room most of the time. We both made peace with that reality years ago," Jason said.

"So you're saying that Richard looks at Micah and thinks he can take him in a fight, so Micah shouldn't be winning Anita either."

"It's more than that. If it was a fight with referees, Richard would win; I think Micah would concede that," Jason said.

Nathaniel and I nodded.

"But if the fight was for real, for dominance

of an animal group, Micah would win," Jason said.

"But wait, how?"

"He'd kill Richard," I said.

Envy looked at me. "Because he sees Richard as a rival for you?"

"No, Micah kills for the same reason I do in a fight, because we're too small not to. If we weren't willing to be more ruthless than a bigger opponent, then we'd both have died years ago."

"Are you serious?" she asked.

"Absolutely," I said.

"He hates Micah the most, because Richard knows he should be able to win the fight, and at some level he knows he wouldn't," Jason said.

"Why wouldn't he?" she asked.

"Because Richard would hesitate going for the kill," I said.

"But if Micah killed Richard, wouldn't you be upset? Wouldn't you blame Micah?"

"You mean if Richard pushed it and Micah finished it, would it mess up our relationship?"

"Yes."

"It would be hard, but I'd understand why Micah did it."

"I don't love Richard, but if Micah killed him, I'd have a hard time getting over it."

"One of the reasons Richard isn't my main lover is that he didn't approve of me being willing to kill to prove my point. He wanted there to be a more civilized way to handle things."

"Anita and Micah are almost equally ruthless," Nathaniel said.

"You're saying they both kill more easily than Richard."

"Oh, hell yes," he said.

"But you're in love with Micah and Anita."

"I am."

"How can you say they're both ruthless, if you love them?"

"Maybe part of what I love is their ruthlessness."

"That's just fucked up," she said.

"Insulting us is not going to win you points," I said.

"Sorry, but I just don't understand. How do you really feel about loving people because they're ruthless?"

"Safer," Nathaniel said.

I squeezed his hand and we exchanged one of those loving looks. The fact that we did it while talking about the fact that we were willing to kill to defend the people we loved was just part of our special little snowflake of a love.

"The weretigers fight among themselves, but we don't kill each other for dominance," she said.

"You're gold clan, which means there were never enough of you to risk death. You weren't allowed to kill each other over dominance," I said.

"There still aren't enough of us to just kill each other over stupid things like this."

"But there are lots of werewolves, and wereleopards," Jason said.

"I don't understand," she said.

"It's a difference in culture between the animal groups. Tigers are matriarchal, which means the leaders don't fight and kill each other to lead; they have champions for that, or enough psychic powers to just overpower everyone in the clan," I said.

"Leopards don't kill each other as much as the wolves do," Nathaniel said.

"So why does Micah kill so easily when he's a wereleopard?" she asked.

"Because Micah came up through a mixed animal group that was run like lions, wolves, and hyenas, which are three of the most violent subcultures we have," Jason said.

I looked at him. "You've talked to Micah about this, haven't you?"

"Here's this new guy in town who's an inch shorter than me and is everyone's dominant leader. I wanted to know how he did it."

"So you could do it, too?" I asked.

He shrugged, grinned, and then it faded to a smile, his eyes not exactly happy. "I don't want it bad enough to do what Micah and you do. I acknowledged that, and moved on."

"One of the few reasons that we would kill one

of our own was if they picked a fight and killed another golden tiger," Envy said.

"The wolves allow you to tap out of a fight before you get killed, but it's up to the winner to grant mercy or take your life," Jason said.

"How have you survived?" Envy asked.

"Most people in our pack like me."

"So they don't want to hurt you," she said.

"And I'm not high enough in the pack structure, so fighting me won't gain them anything."

"And when death is a possibility, there has to be something to gain," she said.

"Yes, or you have to hate someone enough to risk it."

She shivered. "God, that is barbaric."

"Richard prefers fights to be less than lethal, and if he thinks that you killed when you didn't have to, you get punished, so it's a softer pack structure than some," Jason said.

What he didn't say out loud was that I was the pack's Bolverk, the doer of evil deeds. I was Richard's punisher, his threat to bad little werewolves; in effect, I enabled him to keep his conscience and hands cleaner. I hadn't taken the job to help Richard. I'd taken it to keep my friends like Jason, and others, safe from the other wolves, and from out-of-town werewolves trying to move in on our local pack, because Richard's reputation was too soft.

Now it wasn't a problem. Micah's reputation and mine combined meant that animal groups that wanted to try to take over other cities stayed the fuck away from St. Louis. There were easier ways to die than coming here, and no, I didn't feel bad about that. I'd seen too many people die because of territorial disputes between animal groups, or even vampires. We'd put a big sign over our territory saying, *Nothing here is worth dying over, but if you insist, we will fucking kill you.*

Harsh, maybe, but a scary reputation was about what you needed in the lycanthropy community—vampires, too. Publicly, we were all civilized; privately, not so much, or not always.

Domino walked in with his black-and-white curls

still damp from the shower. The hair showed his mixed heritage, black tiger clan and white, but his eyes were pure black tiger, the color of fire: orange, red, bright, hot tiger eyes that couldn't pass for human. They were such a startling color that it took a minute to see that he was handsome in his own right, and not just his bicolored hair and fire-colored eyes. He was five-ten, five-eleven, and was decked out in what had become the unofficial bodyguard uniform: black T-shirt, black pants, black shoes (usually boots), and weapons. Since we were in the house and didn't have to worry about strangers, his shoulder holster complete with .45, extra ammo, and even his backup gun were all visible, if slightly camouflaged in black on black, like dangerous chameleons trying not to be seen in the bright, sunny kitchen.

He came over to me and gave me a kiss, because the rule was if we were sleeping together we could do the usual kiss as a greeting. The fact that we'd woken up together and already had sex, with Nathaniel joining in, meant we could have skipped the greeting, but I knew Domino wouldn't. He didn't get enough time with me to suit him, so he'd take all the attention he could get, and give. I didn't hold it against him. I didn't even blame him, but part of me felt the pressure from Domino and some of my other weretigers. A near-constant push to have more of me, more time, more love, more sex, and there just wasn't any more of me to give to anyone. The sex was great, but I couldn't be the emotional caretaker of this many people, which was why I'd encouraged some of them to find other partners to date-date. Domino hadn't dated anyone else yet.

He turned from me and stared down at Envy. "Please, move," he said.

"Why?" she asked, and took a sip of her tea as if to prove how cozy she was.

"Because until someone enters this room who is more intimate with Anita than I am, I get to sit on the other side of her, that's what we worked out."

"I know she's the Queen of Tigers, even I feel the draw of her power, but really, you would all think she's the only pussy"—and she put a little too much pause between—"cat in the world, the way all of you chase after her."

"You're in my seat," Domino said, quietly.

"This can't be your seat; you're not over here much more often than I am." Her voice was bland, but the point was sharp, because since it was her first time staying over here, it implied that Domino was even less in my life than was true, which was little enough.

He stiffened, his whole body coming to a sort of involuntary attention.

I leaned around Domino so that I could look Envy in the face and said, "You're in his seat. Move."

She frowned, that beautiful face going all petulant on me.

Jason said, "I thought you and Domino were friends."

"Friendly," she said.

"Friendly," he said.

"Then be friendly," Jason said.

Envy sighed heavily and rolled those pretty blue eyes, but she got up so that Domino could sit beside me. I expected her to take the seat beside Jason, but she didn't. She walked all the way around the table and put that extra sway into her walk like Nathaniel had done. She wasn't a stripper or dancer of any kind, but she was a wereanimal, and they knew how to move so that any man, or woman, would wonder if those swaying hips would be as good in reality as they were in the advertisement.

I had enough memories, thanks to being metaphysically linked to so many men, to appreciate that sway as the white T-shirt fluttered just below her ass, so that you could almost see something, but not quite. If I'd had the penis that my memories required, I might even have been interested, but girls as sex objects puzzled me, and though I could admire Envy's physical beauty, it didn't move me, or make me want to explore it.

She finally sat down, then had to have Jason pass her the tea mug she'd abandoned. She took another sip of her mint tea and watched Domino slide his arm across my shoulders with a look that matched her name. In that moment I knew she had a crush on

Domino, or was at least looking for him to supplement once she dumped Richard. Did Domino know, or was he oblivious, or had he already turned her down? Did that explain her overemphasis on the "friendly," that she'd wanted to be more than friends, but he'd said no?

I rubbed my free hand across my forehead. Trying to manage this many people was a pain in the ass, but it usually hit me as a headache when I started overthinking it. They were adults, for the love of God; they should be able to handle this, right?

Nathaniel leaned in and kissed my cheek. "You okay?"

"Sure," but I was tense as I tried to lean into Domino's arm over my chair back. I suddenly didn't want him touching me, felt suffocated by so much attention. What you'll enjoy from someone you're in love with just hits you as clingy from someone you think of more as a sex buddy. Jason was my friend with benefits for real, because he was one of my best friends and the sex didn't seem to mess that part up, or make us want to have more from each other emotionally. He was probably the least complicated lover

I had in some ways; in other ways he was just a different kind of complicated, but then weren't we all.

"Now that the gang's all here, why are we here? Jason mentioned something about the rough sex being part of the reason for this informal meeting. Can you elaborate on that, Jason?"

"Let's go with Domino and Envy's agenda item first," he said, and gave a half smile with it.

"There's an agenda with line items?" I said.

He laughed. "You should see your face, so woebegone."

"I hate meetings." I brought both my hands up to raise my coffee to my mouth. I didn't want to touch anyone right that minute. I felt like they were ganging up on me, managing me, and I didn't like it.

Nathaniel put his hand on my thigh underneath the table, rubbing gently on it through the silk of my robe. I fought the urge to push his hand away. I wanted him to touch me, but I didn't like realizing that everyone at this table knew the topic of conversation except me.

Domino began to rub my shoulders, fingers

finding the bare skin of my neck underneath my hair, kneading the suddenly tense muscles, then moving upward just past the hairline so he could snake his fingers up to knead, and press, and let me feel the strength in his hand in that sweet spot where neck and skull merge. It damn near rolled my eyes back into my head, and did make me close my eyes.

Nathaniel's hand pressed harder, proving that there was strength in his fingers that he didn't normally use, but it was still there. They both tightened their grip at the same time and I had to fight not to react more to it than was polite at breakfast. Someone took my coffee cup out of my hand, or I'd probably have dropped it.

Nathaniel loosened his grip on my thigh and then Domino moved his hand back to just hugging the back of my shoulders. This time I slumped into the curve of his arm, snuggling against his body. I could snuggle tighter because he hadn't put his body armor on; most of the guards didn't bother unless they were going to work with me. He lowered his grip so that he was actually partially supporting me, or I might have slithered out of the chair and into the floor; silk is slippery when your muscles go all liquid.

"Wow," Envy said, "that was . . . wow."

I tried to look at her, but my eyes still weren't focusing just right. I started to try to fight free of that warm, afterglow sensation, but Nathaniel stroked my thigh, gently, and said, "It's okay, Anita, just relax into it."

I started to do what my beloved pussycat's voice told me, and then Envy kept talking and I needed to pay attention. I fought my way through to the surface of all that relaxation, and yummy reminders of earlier this morning, and just . . . They'd hit two of my happy trigger spots, and with the right people, under the right circumstances, it unmanned me, or would that be unwomaned me?

"Can you actually hear me?" she asked, and lowered her face down to peer at me.

I was still snuggled into the corner of Domino's body, his grip across my shoulders holding me in place. The press of his shoulder holster and extra ammo on his belt wasn't uncomfortable; it was actually sort of reassuring. When you hang around with as many dangerous people as I do, the guns and stuff are just part of it all. I wrapped my arms around his waist to help hold myself up, and wrapping my arms around his waist wasn't a bad thing. It helped continue to ease that tension that had tried to assert itself and make me start tearing at everything, and everyone, around me. Rage had been almost my only emotion once, and it was still comforting in that dysfunctional way in which people will prefer something unpleasant, but familiar, to something pleasant, but unfamiliar. Sometimes I thought I'd been pushed so far outside my comfort zone that I'd break, and other times I realized that comfort zones were more like prison bars; they protected you, but they also trapped you. I didn't want to be trapped, not even by myself.

"Yes," I said, voice a little thick and almost sleepy sounding. I cleared my throat and tried again. "I hear you, Envy."

"If Richard put his hand back there and pulled your hair, would you enjoy it?"

I blinked at her, studying the intelligence in her gaze,

the force of will that was in there. Those were the things that made Envy work for Jean-Claude and for Richard; passive wasn't something either of them enjoyed.

"Under the right circumstances, yes," I said.

She shook her head, raised her tea as if to drink it, and then put it back down untouched. "It just hurts when he does it to me."

"Then he shouldn't do it," I said.

"It's like he needs to do it to someone, or with someone."

"He does."

"Why?" she asked.

That made me frown and have to straighten up from the extreme cuddle position I was in, as if I couldn't think as deeply sitting like that. I patted Domino's thigh, letting him know that I wasn't mad, just needed to sit up. I took Nathaniel's hand off my thigh and into my hand, letting him know, too, that I was all right, and that I wasn't going to let my discomfort get out of hand and make me lash out again; that was childish, and I wasn't a child anymore.

"Can I take this one?" Jason asked.

"Be my guest," I said.

"Enjoying pain with your pleasure is something either you get, or you don't. If you get it, then you don't really need it explained, because you know how good it feels, and if you don't get it, then no amount of talking is going to convince you it makes sense."

"Sounds like you've practiced that speech," I said.

He frowned, and it seemed to dim his light all the way through. "I've been trying to explain it to J.J."

"Not going well, I take it?"

"No."

"Don't tell me you can't explain it to me, that is not an answer," Envy said.

"It's like trying to explain the color red to someone who's color-blind. You can tell them red is hot, bright, use any word you want, but it won't really explain to them what the color looks like, it'll still look sort of gray to them," I said.

"That's not an answer either," she said.

Nathaniel said, "You see bondage as an extra, something to add spice in the bedroom, right?"

She nodded.

"For some of us it's not spice, it's the vegetables and fruit."

"What?" she asked.

He sat forward in his chair, using his free hand to gesture as he spoke, the other hand still in mine. "Think of sex, intercourse, as the meat, but if you eat just meat you'll get sick and eventually die from complications of a severely imbalanced diet."

"Okay, I knew that, but I still don't see the analogy."

"We can all have sex without bondage and enjoy the hell out of it, but if we don't have the bondage and submission with it, after a while we get sick and depressed. Sex on its own isn't a complete sex life for us; we need the kink to be happy and healthy, and without it eventually part of us would sort of die inside."

She blinked those big blue eyes at him, and then turned to Jason. "Is that how you feel?"

He nodded.

"I won't ask Anita; the little demonstration said yes for her." She looked at Domino. "Is this how you feel, too?"

"I think I would be okay without the BDSM. I mean, it's not a burning need for me, but Anita is almost never satisfied with straight vanilla in the bedroom."

"I do straight vanilla intercourse sometimes," I said.

He hugged me one-armed and said, "No, you don't; you think you do, but even your vanilla is more like fudge ripple."

I started to get mad about that, and then fought off the urge. My therapist said that the anger had been a coping mechanism since about the time my mother died. The rage had protected me and helped me survive; now I just needed to use it appropriately, and not let it tear my relationships apart like I had for most of my adult life. Old habits are hard to break, but I was trying, and the people I cared about were helping me try harder.

Nathaniel squeezed my hand; he'd noticed my effort, and my success. I looked at him and he smiled at me, that happy, I'm-proud-of-you smile. It made me smile back.

"Okay, what was that just now? I felt Anita's energy, her beast flare, and then it was gone, and now we've got some kind of happy moment going on," Envy asked.

"I'm learning to control my emotions and my inner beast; you know how that works."

She cocked her head to one side just slightly. "This felt different than controlling our other halves. Maybe the anger is what you were controlling, not the beast?"

See, Envy was smart and insightful, and she learned fast. That was also true of her cousin Dev, and it was one of the reasons they were our lovers. Smart isn't just sexy; it's necessary for something this complicated to work.

"Yeah, exactly," I said.

She nodded, more to herself, I think, and then raised her tea and sipped it. She was thinking, you could watch it in her eyes; I liked that.

"Why didn't you like Domino telling you that you don't do straight vanilla?"

"Honestly, because I still don't believe it. I occasionally do straight missionary position with the guys, and I consider that about as vanilla as it gets."

"Not the way you do it," Jason said.

I looked at him and knew it wasn't an entirely friendly look.

He laughed. "Hey, it's the truth."

"What would be straight vanilla missionary then?" I asked.

He looked at the other men, and Envy and I got to see them exchange a series of looks that were suddenly very male, like some arcane handshake that we didn't understand because we didn't have penises.

"What?" I asked.

"Yes, what?" Envy asked.

"Well, you can't try to gnaw your way to freedom with bite marks and fingernails when the guy is on top, that's definitely not vanilla," Jason said.

"I don't mark you up all the time, not if you tell me you have to go on stage that night."

49

"You forget sometimes," Nathaniel said.

I sighed, felt my shoulders begin to slump. Domino hugged me. "It's okay, we're not complaining, but we're all glad you like angles for intercourse that put you farther away from our skin, or I am. I don't really like pain during sex."

"Is it a buzzkill?"

"No, but I won't put myself in a position where you can really sink your teeth in like Nathaniel will, that's all." He kissed my forehead and hugged me again. "Don't make more of it than there is, Anita, it's just differences in what people like. I love that you get so into the sex that you forget and give up your control like that, it's sexy as hell. I love it even more that you forget just as much with me as you do with Nathaniel, or Jean-Claude, or Dev, or Nicky. I love that I can do things to you that you enjoy so much you lose yourself in the sex."

"That's what Jade needs," Envy said.

The topic change was too abrupt for me. "I'm sorry, what?"

"Envy," Domino said.

"No, Domino, we agreed to talk on Jade's behalf, so let's talk about it."

"Talk about what?" I asked.

"Jade is your lover, your only female lover."

"I'm aware of that." I tried not to hunch my shoulders or get embarrassed; I still wasn't completely comfortable with having a woman in my life like a man. Yes, I had metaphysical powers that I didn't have complete control over, and the power that had attracted Jade to me, and me to her, had been a great icebreaker, but it didn't help me deal with the fact that I'd never been attracted to women before, or that when I was most into the sex with her, I kept forgetting I wasn't male. I had centuries of memories in my head from Jean-Claude of the women and men he'd seduced, or who had seduced him, but I didn't have the equipment to act on those memories.

"She needs sex so good she forgets everything."

"She hasn't complained to me," I said, and tried not to sound as grumpy as I felt.

"She wouldn't, would she? She's so happy to be

free from the master vampire that tormented her for centuries that anything is a step up."

"He was an evil bastard to her."

"She's happy, Anita. She loves being with you and she's beginning to trust men again thanks to Domino, Nathaniel, and Jean-Claude, but she still prefers women, and you're her only woman."

"I've offered that she should find another woman if she wants to."

"Neither Domino nor Jade has found other lovers. Of all the tigers that are bound to you, they're two of the few that haven't gone elsewhere."

"Is that like a black tiger clan culture thing?" I asked, and looked at Domino as I said it.

"I don't know. I was raised by the white tigers. Crispin and I were raised together, but he's found other lovers," Domino said. He'd been a foundling taken in by the white tigers, and had actually never been with another black tiger until Jade. We'd all believed the entire clan had been wiped out.

"So why haven't you?" I asked.

"Jade and I both believe that if we find other people, you'll see it as delegating us to them. You won't feel you have to date us, because we'll be dating other people. We've seen you do it with others, Crispin included."

I thought about that for a moment. Was that true? Was my encouraging them to find other lovers a way of getting them out of my bed, if not my life?

"I hadn't realized I was doing that, but no one person, not even me, can truly date this many people. I can fuck, but I can't do the emotional stuff, the cute stuff, the things that really make it a relationship; there just isn't enough of me to go around like that. I'm feeling pressured by everyone to take care of them, and I've reached a limit. I can't take care of this many people as intimately as most of you want me to, I just don't know how to do that. I asked Jean-Claude and even he didn't know how to have real relationships with this many people, and he's been a ladies' man, and a gentlemen's man, for centuries."

"I hadn't really thought about it from that

perspective. I don't think . . . no, I know I couldn't date this many people, but they're all metaphysically tied to you and Jean-Claude and Micah, and there's no untying those bindings except by death," Envy said.

"Anita cut the tie between Jade and her first vampire master," Domino said.

"Yes, but Anita is the Mother of the Dawn, the Queen of Tigers; she breaks servant from master the way that the old Queen of All Darkness did. Even the Queen never broke bonds between herself and any of her own servants," she said.

"So short of death or a metaphysical miracle, the bonds between Anita and all of us are immobile, unbreakable," Jason said.

"Yes," Envy said.

"I'm saying here out loud today that I can't cope with this many people, not and do a good job of dating them, caring for all their needs. Hell, if I hadn't been metaphysically screwed over, I wouldn't have chosen most of the people I'm having sex with, not that it's not great sex," I said, kissing Domino on the cheek, "but it's like I'm suddenly insanely attracted to people I don't have much in common with, so the sex is mind-blowing, but the conversation in between not so much."

"The *ardeur* is like a date-rape drug that doesn't go away," Envy said.

"Not my favorite analogy, but yeah," I said.

"But this drug affects both parties," Jason said.

"Not always. I talked about it with Jean-Claude, and the originator of the *ardeur* as a vampire ability, Belle Morte, was never affected by it; she was more like a contagion."

"Beautiful Death," I said, "making people sick with desire."

"More like addicts," Jason said.

Nathaniel and I nodded. "*Addicted to love* isn't just a song lyric," I said.

I turned to Domino. "Do you crave me like that? I mean, do the others who have found other lovers jones after sex with me like a junkie?"

"Sometimes."

I felt terrible then.

"Wait, but Anita doesn't crave them the same way, or she wouldn't have to ask that question."

"When the *ardeur* first came for me I had almost no control over it, so I was bound as tight as the people I fed on, but I got more control of it and I could protect myself from falling in love."

"I got here too late," Domino said, and kissed me again to take some of the sting out of the words.

"I'm sorry," I said.

Nathaniel leaned in from the other side and kissed my cheek. "I'm glad I got here early."

"It's not just the *ardeur*, Anita. I've known you longer than Nathaniel, and I was around when the *ardeur* rose, but we're not in love, or addicted to each other," Jason said.

"You were terrified of being consumed by love, and when you became my wolf to call, I sort of incorporated that into the mix, so we were both more free of the emotional stuff, or that's what Jean-Claude thinks made the difference."

Jason nodded. "Makes sense. You get some

personality traits that seem to switch bodies when you make someone your wereanimal or vampire to call. Jean-Claude has talked about that; he's more ruthless since he merged with you, and Richard got your anger for a while, so I'm glad you learned to take that back. Our wolf king would have killed someone if he hadn't learned to give up the fits of rage."

"I got Jean-Claude's *ardeur*, his ability and need to feed off lust, and Richard's craving for flesh, and both their cravings for blood."

Envy shuddered. "You don't get to pick and choose, do you?"

"Not at all," I said.

She shivered again. "That could go so badly."

"I've thought of that. It's one of the reasons that I've decided my dance card is full. We've been lucky so far, but eventually I could get a piece of somebody who is really bad and then our happy little poly tribe could go to hell in a big way."

"Is it a happy poly tribe? Are you happy?" Domino asked.

I turned and looked up into those eyes the color of fires and spectacular sunsets. "Yes. Yes, I am happy, happier than I've ever been before."

He smiled a little. "Good, I'm glad."

"I won't ask if you're happy, because I know you want more of me than I have to give, and I'm sorry for that, Domino. I would set you free if I could."

"If he were just addicted to the *ardeur*, you could, or he could sort of detox the way Requiem did, but I know what it's like to be your wolf to call, and he's your tiger, and we're yours forever. Even if we move across the country you can still call us to your side," Jason said.

"Are you thinking about moving across the country?" I asked.

He gave a little shrug. "If J.J. and Freda and I could work things out, maybe, and if Jean-Claude and you would allow it."

"I don't like the 'allow' part," I said.

"Jean-Claude is the vampire king of the United States," Envy said. "Jason is his *pomme de sang*, his apple of blood, and he's your wolf to call; he has to have permission from both of you to move. Anyway, who is Freda?"

"Jean-Claude has enough wereanimals to donate blood now. It's not like in the old days when him having this little werewolf to feed off of was important for his power base. And Freda is J.J.'s girlfriend."

"So if you, J.J., and Freda can work this out, you'll move to New York?"

"Maybe. I mean, she's in one of the top dance troupes in the country; I can't force her to give that up."

"I love that you're willing to relocate for your girlfriend," Envy said. "Most men expect the woman to do the career compromising."

"I'm an exotic dancer, it's not a career."

"You're very good at your job," I said, "and you manage the club most of the time."

"J.J. is talking to the dance company she's in about Jason maybe trying out for them," Nathaniel said.

I looked from one to the other. "Wow, Jason, just wow, that's awesome; would you be the first lycanthrope allowed in an all-human dance company?"

He nodded.

"That would really help lycanthropes be more accepted," Envy said.

"It's a great opportunity," I said. "I'll miss you like hell, but I've never seen you as happy as you are with J.J., so what can I do to help?"

He smiled at me, not his usual teasing smile, but the one that was just him, just our friendship. "First, we all think if you maybe had more experience with women, or could talk to someone about having female lovers, you might be able to help Jade feel more a part of things."

I raised eyebrows and looked across the table at Envy. "Are you volunteering to mentor me?"

"Me, no," Envy said, shaking her blond hair hard.

"Then why are you here today? Domino is the only other black tiger in our group, so he and Jade are pals, but you're golden tiger, which makes you a totally different clan."

"I'm a female weretiger, and the only one you have other than Jade, so she talks to me. I'm with

Jean-Claude and Richard, so she sees our positions as similar: We're lovers, but not the beloved of our lovers."

I tried to roll that sentence around in my head, gave up, and said, "So you're here as Jade's friend?"

"Yes, I am."

"Okay. But you aren't volunteering to teach me? Honestly, I'm not offering either; nothing personal, but Jade is confusing me enough I don't need to add more girls. Hell, I don't even need to add more boys."

"I've never actually been with another woman, so I'm not mad at you that you're puzzled about having a female lover, but you do have sexual contact with Jade; we just thought another woman with more experience in the area might be helpful."

I looked at Jason. "You're not offering some fantasy where you just add me to you and J.J. for a threesome, are you? Because if that's it . . ." I looked at him harder.

He grinned and then laughed. "No, I'm not, though if it's on the table, I wouldn't say no."

"Nothing personal to J.J., she's beautiful, but I can't sec being with her, just the two of us."

"You went straight to sex, didn't you? It never occurred to you to just talk to J.J. over coffee about it, did it?" Envy said.

I blushed, a little, and shrugged. "Am I supposed to have a little bisexual coffee klatch?"

"That might help, but that wouldn't solve my problem," Jason said.

"Which problem?" I asked.

"You can't make Freda hate me less, or stop being jealous of J.J., but you could help me explain rough sex to my girlfriend."

"How?" I asked, and the one word dripped with suspicion.

He grinned, and then his face sobered, happiness gone like a switch, on/off. It hurt me to see him like that.

"Is J.J. really thinking about breaking up with you over the issue?" I asked.

"I'm breaking up with Richard because of it," Envy said.

"No, it's not the same. I don't try to fuck J.J. until it hurts her. She's sort of my version of the human women Richard dates, the ones he wants the white picket fence with, but I need the rough stuff, too. I just know I'm not going to get it with J.J."

"Explain it to her the way you told me, that you'll die without it." She sounded disdainful.

"You don't believe us, why should she?" Jason asked.

Envy opened her mouth, started to say something, stopped, and then sipped her tea; again you could watch her thinking.

"So," I said, "what would help explain it to J.J.?"

"Seeing it," he said.

I glared at him with no chance he'd jolly me out of it. "I'm not that much of an exhibitionist."

"I know, and that's not what I'm asking."

"What exactly are you asking?"

Nathaniel took my hand in both of his, which made me gaze up into those lavender eyes. I wondered if I'd ever look up into his eyes and not be startled by how pretty they were. "We were thinking that you

63

and I would have sex in the room with Jason and J.J. and just let the differences speak for themselves."

I gave him wide eyes.

"It wouldn't be the first time we'd shared a bedroom with another couple, or several, Anita."

"That's for feeding the *ardeur*, or when things get out of hand and we can't control it. I've never agreed to anything like this while sober from the *ardeur*."

"Maybe it's time that you did," he said, softly.

I opened my mouth, closed it, and didn't know what to say. Hell, I barely knew what to think. "Well, fuck," I said, at last.

"That's the hope," Jason said.

Domino said, "Sorry to put a damper on the plan, but Nathaniel and Anita alone don't really go that rough."

The three of us looked at each other. "How rough do you need her to see, Jason?" I asked.

He thought about it for a moment, and then sighed. "Rougher than you and Nathaniel, probably."

"I can do rougher," Nathaniel said.

I patted him. "You can."

"Anita and I are rougher together than you and she alone," Jason said.

"Add Nicky and Nathaniel co-topping me and it's rougher," I said.

Jason laughed. "I want to introduce J.J. to rougher sex, not scare her to death."

"Nicky makes love, too," I said, feeling the need to defend one of my absent lovers.

"I believe you, but I've seen his rough, and something about how tall he is, those massive shoulders, and the edge-play bondage takes him out of the comfort zone for me, let alone for J.J."

Nicky was as blond and blue-eyed as Jason and Envy, but he made everyone here today seem . . . frail. He wasn't the tallest guard we had, but he did have one of the biggest shoulder spreads, and was just one of those big guys who seemed huge, maybe a combination of physical size and personality. He was also an admitted sociopath, which meant his reaction to situations was either socially perfect or so wrong you had no words for it. I loved him, meaning I was in love with him, and he me, which meant he wasn't nearly the sociopath he thought he was, just someone with a childhood background so harsh only Nathaniel's held a candle to it.

"Okay, if Nathaniel and I aren't rough enough, and you don't want Nicky, or I assume anyone else in the room, what are the options?" I asked.

"Since it's Jason's idea of rough that J.J. needs to see, then he and Anita should be the ones demonstrating," Envy said.

We all looked at her; maybe they weren't entirely friendly looks, because she said, "What? That's the logical choice."

I looked at Jason. "Do you think J.J. would be okay watching you and me have actual sex?"

"I don't know. I'll ask, because Envy's right, J.J. needs to see what I'm talking about, not what you and Nathaniel do, or you and Nicky."

And just like that we began to negotiate taking it from an idea to a reality. Every time I thought my sex life couldn't get weirder, or more complicated, I was so wrong.

2

TWO WEEKS LATER, J.J. was able to visit St. Louis. I was incredibly nervous. You'd think there would be a point where I'd had enough sex, broken enough taboos, thrown out enough traditional values that nothing would faze me, but it just didn't work that way. I was disappointed that it didn't work that way; it seemed like if you had thrown all the conventional ideas of sex and relationships out the window, it would make you impervious to being embarrassed, or awkward, but it didn't. I wanted to get angry about that, but I'd expected it to piss me off, so I was ready to fight against the urge to be grumpy. I did pout. I gave myself permission to be grumpy enough to pout about the fact that I felt like I was sixteen again, and had stumbled under the bleachers, tripping over the head cheerleader and star quarterback.

I was nervous and grumpy right up to the moment I saw J.J. step out of the crowd at Lambert Airport. We saw her before she saw us, because we were standing on the raised area that features different local arts and crafts. I was sometimes puzzled by the art, but it was a great way to see over the crowd if you were short like Jason and me. Her face lit up, as if someone had ignited a candle inside her skin so that the happy glow of it filled her and made strangers look at her and Jason, as he ran to her. She dropped her big purse to the floor and flung herself at him. He actually picked her up off the ground, and she bent her knees so he could do so even though she was five foot eight to his five foot four, tucking her feet up so he had all her body weight as they kissed and he turned slowly in place, as if they were dancing to the crowd noise.

Her straight blond hair in its tight ponytail was almost the exact color of Jason's; he was more petite, though her dancer's body honed down to bone and muscle made her seem more delicate, and his bulkier, more weight-lifting body gave him more physical presence, so he seemed bigger, even though she was so much taller.

He sat her down, and she landed with her feet in their flat shoes, in a near–dance position, as if she did it without thinking, the way that I used a gun, so that practice and body memory were always there, waiting to happen. She was dressed as comfy as the brown loafer-style shoes, in soft brown slacks and short tan jacket, over one of those silk sweater-shirts that always seemed too warm to me. She even had a gold-and-tan patterned scarf artfully swirled around her neck and shoulders. It looked great, like a real outfit. I didn't honestly understand accessories once you left shoes and jewelry behind; scarves seriously confused me.

Which is why Nathaniel had dressed me: black skinny jeans tucked into knee-high black boots with a three-inch heel, and a black scoop-neck top tucked into the jeans with a belt that Nathaniel had found in a high-end thrift shop. The belt had a crescent moon for a buckle, and he'd had me throw a tailored leather suit jacket over it all so that it pretty much hid the gun at my back. I didn't go much of anywhere unarmed.

Jason was wearing a baby blue T-shirt tucked into dark blue jeans, with a black belt that matched the boots that peeked out from underneath the jeans. The colors made his eyes even bluer and just looked great on him. Nathaniel was in his own black skinny jeans tucked into knee-high boots that had more buckles and a platform heel, so they looked more science fiction than the sleeker leather of mine or Jason's. Nathaniel had gone for a black T-shirt tucked in, showing his silvery belt buckle that was shaped like a crescent moon/sun. I hadn't noticed that he'd managed to match even the belt buckles until we'd arrived at the airport. We looked like we were going to a Goth nightclub, or to be extras in some futuristic but unrealistic movie where all the dangerous people wore black and looked cool. I would have protested, but honestly most of our dressy-casual clothes were black with a little red, purple, and blue mixed in here and there.

Nathaniel was holding the black leather suit jacket that Jason had worn over his baby blue shirt, because it was really too hot for leather yet, and he'd wanted his hands free to greet his girl. That's what she was; J.J. was Jason's girl. It was there in their faces, how they touched, and in the nearly identical blue of their eyes. They did look eerily alike, and we'd come to find out they shared a great-great-great-grandfather, as did a lot of people from a certain section of Asheville, North Carolina. Legally, most of the blond, blue-eyed women I'd met on my one trip home to see Jason's family weren't related to him, or to each other, but their shared ancestor had been a very busy and immoral preacher, and apparently he'd been at least as charming as Jason, which was pretty damn charming, or maybe more so, which was frighteningly charming.

They turned toward Nathaniel and me, and they

were just so darn happy that suddenly I didn't feel awkward or stupid. I just wanted Jason not to lose this, not to lose her.

"You both look great," J.J. said, hugging Nathaniel and planting a light kiss on his cheek. She turned to me and we hugged. She was five inches taller than me, but she was so tiny through the waist and ribs that she hit my radar as dainty. We pressed cheeks together more than kissed, because though she was wearing her usual neutral lip gloss, I was wearing my usual deep red lipstick and I'd learned that it overwhelmed or looked odd intermingled with other women's lipsticks.

"Nathaniel picked the clothes, so if we look good it's his fault," I said, with a smile.

She smiled a little broader. "Trust me, Anita, it isn't all Nathaniel's clothes choice that makes you look amazing in the outfit."

It took me a moment to think it through and realize that J.J. was saying my body looked good in the clothes, and that was from working out in the gym.

"Thanks," I said.

"I wish I could have your curves and be in shape enough to dance."

Jason hugged her. "I like your curves."

She laughed. "I know you do, but mine are like a drive in the country; Anita's are like a roller coaster."

Jason's eyes sparkled as he looked at me, his face alight with some thought, and just like that I knew that whatever was about to come out of his mouth was something I wasn't going to like, or would be at least teasing.

"Would it piss you off if I said it's a hell of a ride?"

"Yes," I said, and gave him very serious eye contact out of my dark brown eyes. Brown eyes may not look as cold as blue or gray can, but I find that a mean look works just fine.

"Then I won't say it," he said; then he laughed, J.J. joined him, and finally Nathaniel did, too.

I rolled my eyes at all of them.

J.J. didn't have any other luggage. It was a quick two-day trip, and apparently everything she needed was tucked into the huge purse on her shoulder. It was impressively light packing, and I said so.

"After you've been on enough dance tours, you learn to pack light," she said.

It made sense, and she talked about the current production she was practicing for, and the season so far for the dance company. She asked how Nathaniel's and my work was going in the car. I drove, Nathaniel had shotgun, and the two lovebirds got the backseat of my SUV. It was very ordinary small talk except for our jobs being sort of cool, or unusual—a ballerina, a U.S. Marshal with the preternatural branch, a dancer and assistant manager of a strip club, and an exotic dancer at that club.

It felt a little like we were talking around the elephant in the living room. I wanted to point at it and say, "Look, look, an elephant!" I both wanted to talk about the sex and the issues surrounding it, and desperately wanted to ignore it. I think everyone else was actually just talking like friends. I always wanted to either sort of pretend sex and kink issues didn't exist, or take them so head-on that it was jarring to everyone else involved. I seemed to have only two speeds on problems that hit me emotionally, either putting my fingers in my ears and going la-la-la, or picking up an axe and attacking the issue. It wasn't actually a comforting approach for me or the people I loved, but it was what I had for coping mechanisms. I hoped someday to have more middle ground, but right now, I didn't. I was horribly torn between wanting to never bring up the subject of why we were all dressed up to greet J.J. at the airport, and wanting to yell, *Is anyone else nervous, or is it just me?*

Nathaniel reached over and started to rub lightly on my neck as I drove. "You okay?"

I nodded, not trusting myself to speak without being rude or too abrupt. A lot of people take too much directness as rudeness, especially from a woman. I'd like to say it's not sexist, but it is; people expect a woman to have a softer approach to life than most men do. I was so far in the guy camp on my approach to most things that I often came off as harsh even for a man. I didn't mean to, but it happened a lot. I wasn't trying for harsh, I just wanted to say something, or do something, and I wanted to act, not wait until I had to react. Even if by pushing I made the situation worse. It was almost a compulsion that made me want resolution to all uncertainty even if the resolution was negative, rather than wait patiently for a more positive outcome. My therapist and I were working on it, but right at that moment I gripped the steering wheel and just kept my mouth shut; it was the best I had.

J.J. chimed in from the backseat. "Is it just me, or is anyone else nervous about this?"

"Thank God," I said, "yes, me, I am."

"What are you nervous about, honey?" Jason asked, and I knew he was talking to J.J., since he'd never called me honey, ever.

"I'm in love with you, Jason. It means this is more important than just some kinky group sex. You know I'm game, always have been, but never with important relationships. That's always been more straightlaced."

"Maybe that's why they didn't work out," Nathaniel said, turning in the seat so he could look at her.

"What do you mean?" she asked.

"If a person is kinky, and nonstandard sex makes them happy, but they keep putting away the sex they like best every time they're in a serious relationship, then the relationship is doomed, because no matter how much you love your vanilla, you need the other flavors."

"You want the other flavors, you don't need them," she said.

"I used the word deliberately, J.J. I know for myself that if I don't get my bondage and submission needs met I get really unhappy, my energy goes down, and eventually nothing works right. I've accepted that it's a need, not a want, and once I accepted that my life worked better."

"Like me accepting that I liked women, and recently realized that the right man was something I didn't want to live without."

"Like that, yes; you've accepted you're more bisexual than straight lesbian," Nathaniel said.

"Isn't *straight lesbian* an oxymoron?" she asked.

"I don't think so; I've known gay men and women

who were as conservative as any heterosexual. They all try to fit into just one box, and seem to feel that anyone who wants to climb out of that box is wrong, or even evil."

"I don't think Jason needing rough sex is evil."

"But you don't understand why he needs to have it with Anita, right?"

"No offense, Anita, but no, I don't."

"No offense taken; are you saying that you are willing to have rough sex with Jason?" I asked, glancing back in the rearview mirror enough to glimpse her face.

"We have had."

"How rough?" Nathaniel asked.

"Rough," she said.

"No, honey, not by Nathaniel's standards, and not really by Anita's either."

"How rough is rough to them?" she asked.

I concentrated on the road suddenly, just driving, because I didn't know how to answer that. Not without asking them details about the rough sex they'd had that I honestly didn't want to ask.

"It's not just how rough to me and Anita, it's how rough to Jason," Nathaniel said.

"Okay, I'll bite, how rough to all three of you?"

I heard soft movement from the backseat and knew Jason was cuddling her closer in some way. I kept my eye on traffic, but some small sounds you just know.

"I'm not allowed to bite you, remember?"

"I have to perform, Jason, and sometimes my costumes reveal most of my skin."

"And sometimes I can't afford bite marks on me for the same reason."

"So why is it an issue?" she asked.

"You don't want to bite me, and I want to bite you."

"I don't understand," she said.

"I'm hoping you will by the end of the night."

And that was the truth. Some things can't really be explained, they can only be experienced, or at least observed. Tonight was about seeing the truth; I just wasn't sure that I was happy being part of the wildlife being observed.

3

WE WENT BACK to talking about normal things all the way down the long stairs into the underground area below Circus of the Damned. We acknowledged the guards, said hi to the ones who had crossed the line to being friends, and learned more about practice for the new ballet in New York. Nathaniel talked about the dance he and Jason were choreographing for Danse Macabre, which was literally a dance club, not a strip club. I didn't join in the work talk, because most of mine was a little too graphic or involved ongoing police cases; either way it was almost guaranteed to be a buzzkill for J.J. The men in my life were okay with me talking shop—most of the time.

Jason's room was one of the suites complete with bathroom and epic shower. We closed the door to the main bedroom part, and the silence was just the breathing of the ventilation heating/cooling system. All the rooms down here were carved out of a natural cave system, so we didn't actually need a lot of cooling, or heating, but if you did need it, you needed it, and Jean-Claude didn't really believe in skimping. He was spoiling us all, I think.

J.J. kissed Jason and said, "I'm going to freshen up and change into something more comfortable." She walked toward the bathroom, big bag swinging at her side.

I called after her, "Is it really more comfortable, or just the opposite?"

She laughed. "You'll see soon enough."

"Shit, that means I need lingerie, too."

She looked over her shoulder as she opened the door. "Oh, I don't know, you naked would be fine."

She gave me a smile that went with the comment, then was through the door before I had a comeback. Just as well, because I didn't have a comeback. I just stared at the closed door feeling suddenly all deer-in-the-headlights.

Jason hugged me. "Don't get all weird about that, okay? Remember, she likes girls a lot more than she likes boys."

I drew back enough to see his face. "You're not the only boyfriend she's ever had, are you?"

"No, but I am the only serious one."

Nathaniel hugged me from the other side, and for a minute I was held in the warm comfort of a boy sandwich. I liked that, and they both knew it. It helped calm me down.

Nathaniel kissed me. "I'll go get you some lingerie, and shoes."

"I can get it," I said.

He grinned at me. "You'll agonize over the choices, or use it to delay coming back; I'll just pick something awesome for you to wear."

I couldn't argue with his reasoning, so I didn't try.

I could be taught. He went, I stayed, and Jason held me. I realized he wasn't touching just to reassure me.

"You're nervous, too," I said.

"She means more to me than any woman ever has, Anita; it's kind of scary."

"And wonderful," I said, arms around his waist, staring into those spring-blue eyes. He looked worried and had stopped trying to hide it.

"Yes," he said, "wonderful, but still scary."

I hugged him, putting my face against the warmth of his neck. "We got this."

He held me tight, the strength in his arms pressing me against him. "I hope so, Anita. God, I hope so."

I wanted to keep being comforting, but we needed truthful more. I rose back to see his face and said, "I've tried to help Richard make peace with some of his girlfriends and it's never worked well."

"Like Envy," Jason said.

"Yeah."

"I think if Richard had been having rough with you, he'd have behaved himself with Envy."

I shrugged. "He didn't have time to see Envy, date

the new mundane chick, and fit BDSM booty calls into his schedule. He has a full-time job and a lot of family obligations with his parents and siblings in town."

"Richard likes sex rougher than almost anyone else in our group; when you play that hard, you can't skip it."

I agreed. "Not without it coming out somewhere else."

Jason nodded. "Which lost him Envy." His face fell into sad lines.

I moved my hands so I was gripping his shoulders, and I shook him a little. "Snap out of it; we are not Richard. We are all more in touch with our needs, and priorities, than that."

He smiled, and it almost filled his eyes.

"You're getting J.J. and me in one bed at the same time; come on, if you don't make at least one lesbian fantasy joke, I'll be disappointed."

He gave me the full smile then, making his eyes shine with it. "If I said I'd never fantasized about the two of you in bed with me, I'd so be lying."

I hugged him, smiling. "That's my lecherous wolf."

He hugged me back. "Thanks, Anita, for everything."

I wanted to say, *Thank me after this works*, but that would have undone all the reassurance I'd just done, so I just said, "You're welcome."

Nathaniel came back with my clothes and a pair of silk shorts for himself. J.J. opened the bathroom door in a pale-blue baby doll nightie thing. It clung to her body, with touches of lace here and there. She'd combed out her long, straight hair so that it surrounded her face like a shining curtain. She'd also darkened her eye makeup just a little.

All three of us looked at her. Jason said, "You are amazing; that you love me just makes me think better of myself."

She grinned, and it reminded me of Jason. "The look on all three of your faces when I stepped through the door was just about perfect."

"What would have made it perfect?" Nathaniel asked.

"We'll discuss that later; right now everyone else is way overdressed."

"Anita and I will change, and let you guys have some alone time." Nathaniel took my hand and started leading us toward the bathroom and J.J., shining in the doorway.

"Sounds good," she said, and moved so we had room to move past her. We closed the door to the sound of her laughter and the low murmur of Jason's voice.

Nathaniel had chosen a black teddy and a pair of black strappy stiletto heels. The teddy was sheer, so that once I fluffed my breasts into the top part, my nipples pressed against the thin material, and when I turned around using the mirror to see behind me, let's just say it was one of those pieces of lingerie that pretended you weren't nude, but made sure you could see everything, just through a gauze of black sheer.

"I'd have picked something a little less see-through," I said.

"I know, but you won't mind if Jason tears this one off you, and you'd bitch if he tore the silk ones."

"Oh, yeah, we did negotiate that he could tear the clothes off my back."

"You say that like you don't enjoy it, and you do."

I looked away from the mirror so I couldn't watch myself get embarrassed. It was bad enough feeling it; didn't need the visual.

Nathaniel hugged me from behind and turned me so I could see us both in the mirror. "You look fabulous, and you're just competitive enough to want them both to have the same look on their faces as we did for J.J. when you come through the door."

That embarrassed me, too, but for different reasons. "I'm not competitive with Jade."

"You're sleeping with Jade."

"I'm not competitive with Envy."

"No, that's true, which is a little weird, actually."

"Why?"

"Because she's five-eleven, mostly legs, and traditionally model gorgeous; that would sort of freak out most women."

I shrugged with his arms still wrapped around

me. "Her inseam is six inches longer than mine. We're built so differently that it'd be ridiculous to compare us, like making a Clydesdale and a Thoroughbred racehorse race each other. They're both horses, but that's about it."

He laughed, hugged me, and kissed my cheek. "That is the healthiest analogy I've ever heard from any girl. You really don't compare yourself to other people?"

"Not to women who are too different from my body type, no. That wouldn't make any sense. I did it more when I was younger, but I finally realized that trying to compare myself to women who are built tall and leggy is like trying to compete in the gym with the guys who were six feet plus—it's outside my weight limit. I'm a bantam and they're heavyweights, or in the old vaudeville terms for showgirls, Envy is a stallion and I'm a pony. Neither one is better than the other, they're just different."

"Difference can be good."

I nodded, smiling. "It can, and I'm not comparing myself to J.J. either, because she's a ballerina and her body is from some of the most strenuous exercise on the planet. She's a professional athlete; I work out to run away from the bad guys."

"Or chase them down," he said.

"Or that," I said.

"I compare myself to the other dancers, and some of the other men."

I turned so I could look directly at him, rather than at his reflection. "Are you saying you have body issues?"

He shrugged. "A little."

"You are one of the most beautiful men I know, and one of the best lovers ever; how can you have body issues?"

"I strip on stage, Anita. I get customers talking about my body in person and online; it's hard not to be self-conscious."

"So, me pointing out you're beautiful doesn't really help you work the issue," I said.

"No, because the issue isn't about logic, or even reality; it's an issue that's about illogic, and emotions, and the negative voices in everyone's head."

"Everyone has their issues, I guess."

He nodded, and then smiled. "But tonight, we get to have sex in the same room as Jason and J.J., and that totally rocks."

I turned and patted his shoulder. "You are my little voyeur."

"No, I'm your great big voyeur; it is one of my major kinks."

"You're a pretty big exhibitionist, too," I said.

"Yep, and tonight we get to do both. Let me change, and let's go do this."

"You have no qualms about this, do you?"

"If anyone can help J.J. feel comfortable with all this, it's us."

I nodded, because it was reasonable, even logical, but . . . "I'm not a voyeur, or an exhibitionist."

"Not really, but you are two things that will make this work."

"What two things?"

"Jason's friend and lover."

"You got me there," I said.

He started taking off his clothes, and I turned

around so I wouldn't be distracted as he stripped. Him undressing always seemed to make me want to touch him, and tonight we needed to save the distracting touching for group activity. Just thinking that in my head was a little weird. My life; sometimes it amazed me, sometimes it just made me go *Huh?*

4

BUT INSTEAD OF hot monkey sex, we ended up talking. J.J. didn't know me well enough not to ask one question too many. She asked, "What bothers you most about dating Jade?"

It was a list, and the itemized list changed order from day to day. I lay propped up on my side in my see-through black teddy and fuck-me heels talking very seriously. J.J. lay on her back in her blue silk nightie, face intent on mine, listening, nodding, adding a comment here and there.

"So without the *ardeur* binding you to her, you'd never have been attracted to women, at all?" she asked.

I shook my head. "Nope."

"That would be hard, and the memories you have of Jean-Claude and others being with women are all guy memories, so you don't have the equipment to do what you remember."

"Yeah."

Her pretty face was very serious, and watching the intelligence behind her blue eyes made me understand even more why Jason had decided this was the one. Smart is sexy.

"Too much talking, not enough sex," Jason said, from where he was propped beside J.J.

From behind me Nathaniel said, "Agreed."

"How do we stop all the talking and get to the sex?" Jason asked.

I lay back on the bed so I could see them both. J.J. and I watched them go back and forth like a sexy tennis match.

"Pounce," Nathaniel said.

"Pounce?" Jason made it a question with a lift of his voice.

Nathaniel nodded solemnly. "Pounce."

"Cats"—he rolled his eyes—"but it works for me."

They pounced.

5

MUCH LAUGHTER AND giggling later, the boys convinced us both that words were extras we didn't need. I lay on my back, looking down the line of my body at Nathaniel's face as he licked between my legs with long, sweeping strokes of his tongue. He'd unfastened the hidden snap on the teddy to reach me, pushing the cloth up to my waist. J.J. lay beside me with her blue silk pushed up as far, and Jason's face mostly hidden against her body.

I was already making small, eager noises when J.J.'s body spasmed up from the bed as if a string had pulled her upward and held her for a long, impossible moment, her face slack, eyes wide, and then her body began to shake with the force of her orgasm.

Nathaniel hesitated a second, as we both watched her writhe and almost dance over the bed, as Jason kissed and sucked her. Nathaniel brought his longer strokes quicker and more often over that one sweet spot. J.J.'s hand reached out and I found myself holding her hand as that warmth built low in my body, and Nathaniel began to swirl his tongue in nearly circular motions, quick, but pressing a little more firmly over that one spot, each time he licked over it. The pressure and warmth built inside me, low and growing between my legs, until one last lick pushed me over the edge and the orgasm rolled up and over me. My head went back, my spine bowed, and I screamed my pleasure to the headboard.

I felt J.J.'s hand spasm in mine, but it was a distant thing. I clung to her hand as my body bucked and writhed, and Nathaniel kept licking and sucking, helping the orgasm last longer, so that it was wave after wave of pleasure, until my eyes fluttered closed and I was blind from the pleasure of it.

I felt the bed move, a second before I heard, "Trade me." I knew it was Jason's voice. I might have asked what he meant, but I was still quivering on the bed with happy aftershocks.

I felt him lick me, and knew it was him, or rather that it wasn't Nathaniel, before I managed to open my eyes enough to be absolutely sure. He looked up at me with that happy darkness in his eyes, and blue eyes held that dark, just as good as any other color. It wasn't a darkness of hue, but of intention. It was a possessive, a surety, a "This is mine."

I wasn't his, but in that moment I sort of was, and the knowledge of it was there in his eyes. It made me turn my head so I could see Nathaniel with J.J.—we'd negotiated that oral without barrier was okay between us all. J.J. was human, the only full human in the bed, which meant she could catch and carry disease. Whether I was still human enough to do the same remained to be seen, but caution was better. She'd tested clean and hadn't added any new lovers since, so we rolled the dice, pretty sure it was okay. Sleeping with lycanthropes and vampires had spoiled me. They couldn't catch or carry any disease, so fluid sharing wasn't as big a deal. In so many ways, humans were more dangerous.

J.J.'s breathing quickened as her body began to build quickly to the next climax. I tensed up, and Jason noticed enough to draw back and say, "It's okay, Anita, it's not a race."

"Sorry," I said. I had trouble relaxing with another woman in the bed doing certain things, because Domino had discovered I was slower achieving orgasm through oral, especially the second or third time, where most women climaxed faster the more foreplay their partner did. It was also partly a very old hang-up from my ex-fiancé in college, who had made me feel badly that I took so long to come like this, though I'd learned that it was his lack of skill, not my body, that had been at fault. I'd thought I'd exorcised that particular demon, until I started having sex with another woman in the bed; funny what will raise the old ghosts. Domino had asked permission to get advice from Jason, so he knew.

Jason smiled up at me. I expected him to make some teasing remark, but he didn't. "I know it costs you something to include other women; I don't understand it, but I know it does, so thank you."

"You're welcome" seemed a little formal under the circumstances, but I said it anyway.

He grinned up at me, grabbed a pillow, and said, "Make a bridge." I rose up so he could put the pillow underneath me, to help him stay at the angle he needed without hurting his neck.

J.J. made small, eager noises as Nathaniel brought her again. We both looked to that side of the bed, watching our nearest and dearest be all intimate with each other. Then Jason settled himself between my legs and began to lick, suck, and kiss his way over and around me. It felt amazing, but I was distracted by the other side of the bed and J.J.'s breathing already speeding up, again.

Jason bit my inner thigh a little harder than most

people liked it. It caught my breath in my throat and made me stare down at him.

"That's better," he said. "I want more of that look in your eyes." His voice was already a little deeper, from whatever he'd just seen on my face.

He licked and nibbled, and started adding small bites in; sometimes that distracted me from any orgasm, but if the mood was right, it added to it. Jason was a good judge of it. He'd bite, and I'd make a pain noise, not a happy noise, and he'd back off and go back to licking and sucking; then he'd bite on the sides of me, and if that brought happy noises, he'd try biting, semi-gently, over the sweet spot in the center. When my breathing quickened from it, spine arching a little, he bit harder. I cried out from it, and he took more of me into his mouth and shook like a dog with a toy. I screamed my orgasm for him, hands scrambling for something to hold on to, as he worried at me with teeth and mouth, until I waved him off. We had hand signals because sometimes the orgasms left us all wordless while we shook and quivered with the aftermath of it.

He licked me one more time up the middle. It made me cry out, and dragged my upper body off the bed as if someone had pulled me upward by some invisible string, and then cut it to send me collapsing to the bed again.

Jason was above me on all fours, staring down into my fluttering eyelashes. His eyes had gone to that pale spring green of his wolf form. There was something about doing oral sex that way that brought his beast closer to the surface.

"Did she just go from you biting her there?" J.J. asked.

"Yes," Jason said, but he said it while looking into my face.

I fought to turn my head, so I could see her propped up on her elbows, looking at us. Nathaniel lay beside her, one arm thrown across her hips, his face nestled against her body. The look in his eyes was full of that eager darkness, turning them to a deeper violet.

"You enjoyed it," she said.

Jason looked at her then, let her see the wolf eyes.

"Yes," and there was an edge of growl in his voice now.

"You can never, ever do that to me," she said.

"I know," he said.

"Is that what you meant about rough?"

"Part of it," he said.

"What's the other part?" she asked.

"You said no to intercourse with Nathaniel. That leaves you just watching while we fuck."

"You know I'm a voyeur," she said.

"Me, too," Nathaniel said, still cuddled against her body.

"Sometimes I think you'd rather watch than participate," I said.

"Sometimes," he said with a smile, "but not tonight. I want to watch, as foreplay."

"You want to help me demonstrate?" Jason asked with a grin.

"Go, team," Nathaniel said, grinning back.

"The three of you have sex together a lot, don't you?" she asked.

"He's my best friend," Jason said.

"You know, most guys watch sports with their best friends," J.J. said.

"I don't like sports."

"I've done wilder things than this, just never with anyone I cared about," she said.

"You want to back out?" he asked.

She shook her head. "No, I want to watch you fuck."

"Good, because I want you to watch us fuck." He looked down at me again; his eyes were back to human. In fact, a lot of the heat had cooled.

"We talked too long," I said.

He looked down at his body. "You'll have to help get me back in the mood."

"Always glad to help a friend," I said.

He grinned and then laughed. "Then go down on me until I'm hard"—he leaned down and spoke low—"and then let's show J.J. what I mean by rough."

"Let's," I said, and smiled up at him.

6

JASON STAYED ON his knees, and I half sat up so that I could use my hands as well as my mouth. I spilled my mouth over him, sucking him until I could press my lips tight against the front of his body. He was only partially erect, so it was easier to force my mouth over him and hold all of him in my mouth. I played gently with his balls with one hand and kept the other on his waist/butt area, both to touch him and as a sort of balance point.

I kept myself pressed as tight as I could to his body, sucking and rolling him in my mouth, because

I'd learned that as long as I stayed this deep with a man partially soft, he didn't seem to harden as quickly, so I could enjoy the sensation of all of him in my mouth without fighting my gag reflex to do it, but apparently from the outside looking in, it looked even more impressive, because . . .

"How can you deep-throat him that long?" J.J. asked from where she had propped up on the pillows on their side of the bed.

I rolled my eyes toward her enough to see her, but I didn't want to give up my position; I knew that once I went off him long enough to answer J.J., he'd get harder and deep-throating would start to become a challenge. I was enjoying what I was doing and didn't want to give it up yet.

Nathaniel said, "As long as you keep your mouth sealed over him like that, it takes him longer to get fully erect, so the deep-throating is easier."

"Really?" she said.

"Really," he said.

I got my first hint that maybe rough sex wasn't the only thing that J.J. didn't do the same way I did.

I looked up the line of Jason's body, where he knelt above me. We had a moment of eye contact, and the look was enough to let me know that J.J. didn't have my fascination for oral sex, at least not fellatio. It was one of my very favoritest things, but then J.J. had been a lesbian most of her life, so she probably rocked me out of the park on cunnilingus.

Jason's body actually softened a little, as if he were thinking too hard about unpleasant truths, so I redoubled my efforts, sucking and rolling him around in my mouth, one hand coaxing and playing with other bits, nails digging lightly into his ass, as I felt him growing inside my mouth. He started making small involuntary sounds for me, and finally closed his eyes, his head falling forward as he breathed out, "Oh, my God."

Only then did I draw my mouth off him slowly, letting him unfold like magic, until my mouth got to the end, and then I sucked him back inside as quick as I could, but now I had to struggle a little to drive my lips down to retouch his body with the hardness of him not just filling my mouth, but beginning to spill down my throat.

I wrapped my hand around the base of him and began going up and down on him as fast as I could, using my hand as the new stopping point. I still couldn't breathe at the farthest point, but I wasn't staying down that far to feel like I was suffocating. It isn't always a gag reflex; sometimes it's an "I can't breathe" reflex.

"Stop, stop, or you'll bring me," Jason said, voice thick with strain. He groped for the headboard, but he wasn't close enough to reach it. Nathaniel was there to offer a hand and steady him. Sometimes teamwork wasn't about sex; it was about making sure no one falls off the bed.

"Condom," Jason said, and his eyes were closed. He was really fighting his body and his concentration, which meant I'd gone too far with the oral sex. There was foreplay and then there was sex besides intercourse.

"Sorry," I said, and started to get up and reach for the bedside table and the condoms.

"Don't apologize, that was awesome," Jason said, but his voice still held that strained waiting, and his forearm was still corded with muscle as he gripped

Nathaniel's hand, like the ultimate male handshake, except this one was keeping him on his knees, and not collapsed to the bed.

I had to turn around and crawl to the side of the bed, reaching out to the drawer and the condoms. I got a short string out, because it was easier to grab, then crawled back more securely on the bed. I was about to turn around and hand him the condoms, when he said, "Stay there."

"What?"

"Stay right there."

"Why?" I moved enough to glance back over my shoulder at him. His eyes were open now, and they'd bled from human blue to his wolf's pale green. Something about what I was doing had excited him. I started to ask, *What?* and then realized the teddy had worked up around my waist, so I was nude from the waist down except for the stilettos, and his view was of my ass.

"I take it we're doing doggy style," I said.

"Oh, yeah," he said, and his voice was a little lower, maybe with his beast, or maybe just the testosterone that can rush through men at certain moments.

Nathaniel took the condoms from me and handed one to Jason. He unwrapped it, tossed the wrapper off the bed, and began sliding it on. Just watching him putting it on tightened things low in my body and made me fight not to offer him my ass like I was in heat. If it had just been the three of us, I probably would have, but with J.J. watching it felt a little slutty, or animalistic; either way, not in front of company.

"You sure you're okay with this?" he asked, and it took me a second to realize he wasn't talking to me.

J.J. said, "Don't you dare stop now, I loved watching her go down on you."

He smiled at her and turned, with the smile changing slightly as he looked down at me. "Do it, Anita, just do it, don't hold back."

I thought I knew what he meant, because I let myself arch my ass up toward him, my upper body staying against the bed, face buried against the pillows.

"God, I love it when you do that."

He ran his hands gently across me, until I writhed for him, wanting him to finish what we'd started.

He angled himself toward me, and then used his hands to move my hips slightly so the tip of him could find my opening. Just the feel of him entering me brought a soft sound from me. I loved the feeling of that first push inside.

"Wet, but so tight," he breathed as he pushed his way inside, and there was that moment when he was buried as deep inside me as he could get and I felt his body pressed as close against mine as he could get. I loved just knowing that we were married as close as it was possible to be; there was just something about it that floated my boat up, down, and sideways.

He began to pull himself out and then push in, finding a rhythm that was fast, but not as fast as he could be, and nowhere near as rough. I was about to tell him to be rougher, but he found just the right angle and began to pump himself over that sweet spot inside me. I didn't want to protest; I just pressed my face into the pillows and gave myself over to the growing sensation of it. I could feel the delicious weight of the orgasm building as Jason went in and out, over and over that one spot that wasn't actually that far inside, but you just had to find the right angle, and he'd found it.

My breathing started to speed up, and then from one stroke of his body to the next he spilled me over the edge and I was screaming my orgasm into the pillow, driving my body up onto him, as if in the throes of the orgasm I wanted to fuck him faster, harder. He didn't fight what I wanted, just grabbed my hips so that he could get a better hold to pound himself into me, because that's what he did. While I was still riding the orgasm he started fucking me as hard and fast as he could, so that our bodies slapped together. He held my hips tighter so I could no longer move against him, and it was all his body driving us together with a sound as if someone were slapping flesh against flesh, as hard and fast as he could manage it. He was faster and stronger than human-normal, so that was pretty damn fast and hard.

I raised my face out of the pillows so my screams of pleasure were louder, echoing off the headboard, as Jason brought me again and again, and only when my screams had faded to small whimpering sounds of pleasure and I'd started to go boneless sliding back to the bed, not because I wanted to, but because I was beginning to lose control of my body, eyes fluttered closed with the multiple orgasms, only then did he finally thrust himself inside me one long, last time, burying himself as far as he could reach inside me. I felt his body shudder above me, and it made me writhe and make small noises as my body twitched with the pleasure of it all.

I felt him shudder again and half-collapse over me, driving us both into the bed, while he was still inside me. He slipped out by the time we were both flat to the bed, his body still pinning mine, so that I could feel his heart frantic in his chest, the pulse of our bodies roaring with the fierce pleasure of it. I twitched underneath him, unable to move, or open my eyes enough to see, blind with pleasure.

Distantly over the pounding of my own blood in my ears, I heard someone say, "Wow." I thought it was J.J. but wasn't sure, and was pretty sure in that moment I didn't care.

Jason moved slowly, rolling to the side of me,

more a controlled fall than getting up. He patted me clumsily somewhere between my back and my ass. "You're good, good you." His voice was still breathy.

J.J. was talking. I heard her, but it was like I couldn't make sense of it. I tried to move my head and look at her, but that seemed like too much trouble, so I settled for raising a hand. It fell back to the bed without doing much, and then an aftershock hit me, so that I was writhing along the bed and making small helpless noises for a few seconds. Lying there and just enjoying the afterglow seemed like such a good idea, so I did that.

Nathaniel's deeper voice said something like, "Give them a few minutes to recover."

Yes, that. I voted that. Jason's hand patted me again, and I fought to turn my head enough to look at him, but I had so much of my own hair spilled across my face that it was just a shine of his blond hair, and the glow of the lamp on the other side of the bed, so that the world seemed edged with light and I couldn't tell if it was really how the room looked, or if it was still the shiny afterglow;

sometimes it made halos of light around everything, even things that didn't actually have a light shining out of them. Yay, great sex!

I kept waiting for Nathaniel to move closer and touch me, take his turn, but he didn't. When I could move I'd look around and see what was wrong.

"That was incredibly hot, and if I didn't love Jason enough to marry him, I'd just want to climb all over both of you and join in, but . . . I think . . . I think I'm intimidated."

I began to get a clue why Nathaniel hadn't joined us, because he could see J.J. and I couldn't. We could have great sex later; emotional hand-holding sometimes had to be done ASAP, or there was no sex later. That made me fight to turn my head more and raise a clumsy hand to push my hair out of my face so I could see better. The room was all shiny golden light, but I still had trouble focusing beyond the top of Jason's head to J.J., where she sat on the far side of the bed. Nathaniel was nestled in the pillows above us.

Jason found his voice first. "Why? You are great in bed, J.J., and we have amazing sex together."

"I love making love to you, Jason, but it's never like this."

"It is so hot between us," Jason said.

She nodded. "But it's not . . . it's not." She made a vague gesture in our direction.

"Do you understand what Jason meant about rough now?" Nathaniel asked.

She looked at him. "Yes," but her eyes were too wide, and her face too unhappy. This could all go so terribly pear-shaped and blow up the happiness they shared. It was always a danger to show this much of the rest of your life to someone who didn't want to be a part of it; if they freaked out on you, then your two halves of happiness could become one half of happy and another half of serious sad.

I raised my head up enough to say, "Nothing we did takes away from the lovemaking that you and Jason share."

"If this is the kind of sex he wants, I'll never be able to do it."

"I don't want this rough all the time," Jason said. "Most of the time lovemaking is what I want." He sat up, drawing his knees in and wrapping his arms around them. He knew he was in trouble.

"Do you and Anita make love?"

I wanted to say, *Danger, Will Robinson, danger!*

"Mostly we do this, and I share Anita with Nathaniel, or Jean-Claude. I enjoy sharing with another guy."

"Nathaniel was very good at oral; you both need shirts that say, *Oral skills approved by lesbians!*" and she grinned.

Something tight in my chest eased; if she was making jokes, we could work this out.

Jason crawled over the bed toward her. "I love you."

"I love you, too." Her face went serious again.

Jason wrapped her in a hug and kissed her, trying to put more body English into it, but she stopped, and pushed him away enough to study his face. "I get why you want to keep Anita, just for the oral sex alone. She's amazing at it, and I do not like going down on boys that much."

I wanted to ask, *Why not?*, and then thought, *Why not?* "Why don't you like going down on boys?" I asked.

"I like breathing, and my gag reflex is a lot more than yours."

"I used to have more gag reflex."

"How'd you get past it?"

"Practice," I said, and I couldn't help but smile and then look down when I realized I was blushing.

"Lots," Nathaniel said, moving toward me.

"And lots," Jason said.

"Of practice," Nathaniel and Jason said together, and then they laughed that masculine laughter that was usually about girls and sometimes at the girl's expense, but not always. Sometimes it was just a shared buddy happiness that just happened to involve sex.

I let my hair hide my face while I finished blushing. God, would I ever not blush?

"You're blushing," J.J. said. "I wouldn't think this would embarrass you."

"I'm not embarrassed about loving oral sex, but lying here naked in front of Jason's lady love after just fucking our brains out is a little beyond even my usual limits."

"Really?" J.J. asked.

I nodded, and finally looked full at her. Her face was very serious over Jason's shoulder; the back of his body perfectly nude was wrapped in her arms, but it was as if the nudity meant nothing to her, or even really the sex. If the sex wasn't bothering her, what was?

"What's wrong, J.J.?" I asked; once I wouldn't have, but I knew that if this was going to work we had to talk about it, all of it.

"I think I'm trying to process that I'll never be able to meet all of Jason's needs."

"But he'll never be able to meet all of yours," Nathaniel said.

"That's different; he's a boy and I love women."

"Why is it different?" I asked.

She looked at me. "Because I could physically meet his needs that you meet, but he couldn't meet my needs with Freda, he doesn't have the right parts."

"It's not just boy and girl parts," Jason said. "It's different people meet different needs."

"It's a lot more than just preferred genitalia," Nathaniel said.

"What do you mean?" she asked.

"I'm probably the most truly bisexual person in this bed, so for me it's really not just the genitalia, but each person in my life meets different needs that no single person, or even two individual people, could meet," Nathaniel said.

"Examples," she said.

Jason settled behind her so that he was cradling her in her blue silk nightie. It meant they were both mostly covered, and Nathaniel still had his silk shorts on, which meant I was the only truly nude person in the bed; how did this happen? I was suddenly cold, or modest, or both, and I got up enough to slip under the sheet.

Nathaniel scooted down to slip under the sheets, too, so he could wrap me in his arms, so we were almost mirroring how Jason and J.J. were cuddling, except we were lower in the bed and propped against the pillows while they were sitting up more.

Nathaniel held me in the warmth of his arms and the solidness of his body as he said, "Jason is my best friend, Anita is the woman I love most in the world, Micah is the man, Jean-Claude is our master and him taking blood as foreplay with all of us in the bed is amazing, Asher is my dominant for bondage and sometimes for rough sex, Cynric is the little brother I never had, Nicky is brother and friend and I'm learning to really enjoy co-topping Anita with him, Dev is completely comfortable with his bisexuality, and that's nice just to have someone else who feels the same way, and I'll leave out everyone who doesn't have some sexual connotation for me, but there are friends and family who I'll never get naked with that are important to me and help make my life work."

"How is your little brother a sexual connotation?" she asked.

I fought the urge not to squirm, because I had issues with Cynric. Sin was what he wanted to be called, not Rick. He was nineteen now and a senior, but I still had trouble with the age difference between him and me. I would miss him if he left my life, but he still hit all sorts of issues for me. I gave my best blank cop face and let Nathaniel talk. We were shoveling J.J.'s issues right now, not mine.

He hugged me tighter, as if he felt that small body

movement and understood it all. "I like watching Cynric have sex with Anita, and I enjoy sharing her with him, just the three of us, or sometimes with other people joining in."

"One of my biggest fantasies is sharing Jason with another woman, but I have a sister and I can't imagine sharing Jason with her," J.J. said.

"Maybe if Cynric and I had been raised together from childhood it would be different, but he was seventeen when we met, and he's a younger brother for me, but I've never thought of him as anything but an adult, younger than me, but still a person and not a kid."

She nodded. "That makes sense, I guess, so he's family of choice, not of blood?"

"Yes," Nathaniel said, laying a soft kiss against my cheek. I caught a faint hint of J.J.'s scent; it wasn't bad, just different, just not me. His face was still shining from going down on both of us. I wrapped his arms closer around me and let the surety of him help me feel better about so many things.

"If Freda weren't so insanely jealous of Jason,

things would be so great. How did you find so many people that aren't jealous?"

"Jean-Claude has a reputation; if you want to be in his inner circle, you'd better not be the jealous type," Nathaniel said.

"Jean-Claude is amazing, and he seems to override your sexual preferences, as if everyone should want him," she said.

"It's part of his charm," I said.

"It's more than that; Jean-Claude is all about sex and sensuality, and just like Jason doesn't like men, but would do Jean-Claude, I don't like men much, but yeah, I see the appeal."

"Most people see the appeal of Jean-Claude," I said.

She nodded, and settled more comfortably back against Jason, as if some tension had gone out of her. I wasn't sure why she was relaxing, but we seemed to be winning, so I'd take it.

"Everyone told me that when I found the right person I'd be happy being monogamous, but you're telling me that that didn't work for you guys either."

"Nope," I said.

"No," Nathaniel said.

Jason kissed her cheek. "I've tried just one woman at a time, but it never worked for long."

"I've been with Freda for two years."

"Have you been monogamous?" I asked.

She shook her head. "I never wanted that, and I made it clear that I might never be okay with just one-on-one. I've continued to date, but less and less, because she made it such a pain. It just wasn't worth the jealousy and fights, until I met Jason again." And she turned in his arms so she could look back over her shoulder at him. They shared the kind of smile that Hollywood tells us we all should be looking for, and it made me happy to see it.

"Glad to know I'm worth fighting for," Jason said, and kissed her.

She kissed him back, and then said, "If I'd known about polyamory in high school, we might have kept dating, but everyone tells you to choose."

"You told me you were a lesbian; I respected that, but it meant dating each other was done."

"I thought I had to choose one sex to date, one

person to love until death do we part, and it never worked for me."

"Or me," he said.

"I think Freda is monogamous and just pretended not to be until we moved in together."

"Do you still love Freda?" Nathaniel asked.

She didn't answer right away. "I don't know, I thought I did, before she was so ugly about Jason. I mean he's a man, Freda doesn't have the same parts, so I thought she'd be less jealous than she was of other women, but it's worse."

"Was it worse at first, or only after you got serious about Jason?" Nathaniel asked.

She thought about that, and finally said, "Actually, from the beginning, she seemed to feel like I was betraying the lesbian sisterhood. I'd always told her I was bisexual, but I think she thought it was just something you say to be hot, or edgy. I'm not just gay, I'm bi, you know?"

I felt Nathaniel nod at the same time I did. He said, "It's hot for women to be bi, but it's not for men."

I hugged his arms tight against me. "It is incredibly hot when men are bisexual!"

He laughed, hugged me, and snuggled over me until we could kiss. "You think so, but most women are weirded out by it, and gay men think you're just afraid of admitting that you're gay, and straight men think you are gay, and after their virtue."

Jason nodded. "I'm not really bi, at all, but because I'm Jean-Claude's *pomme de sang*, everyone thinks I am."

"His apple of blood," J.J. said. "You're his main blood donor."

"Actually *pomme de sang* is more than that, it's almost like a mistress in the old-fashioned sense of keeping them in style," I said.

She nodded, face serious again. "Jean-Claude would need a new *pomme de sang* if Jason moves to New York."

"I was Anita's *pomme de sang* once, but when I became her boyfriend she didn't get a new one," Nathaniel said.

"But you're still in her bed so she can feed on you.

Jason will be too far away for Jean-Claude to feed on him."

"One problem at a time," Jason said. "First, do you understand what I meant by rough now?"

"Yes," she said, and hugged him around herself. She was back to looking unhappy again.

"And you're okay with me having rough with Anita?"

"Okay, not entirely, but will I make you give her up? No. Honestly, if we all agreed to gentler sex for me, I'd love to have my fantasy come true with Anita and you."

I stiffened a little, and Nathaniel helped me hide my face by bending over me and turning me around so we could have a longer and more passionate kiss. I could taste J.J. on his lips, in his mouth, mingling with the taste of my own body. It made me start to pull away, but it wasn't a bad taste, just . . . I'd never kissed him before when he tasted of another woman. Apparently, my issues with women in certain areas had shown on my face, even before I tasted J.J. I appreciated the help at hiding it, but he gazed down at me as I drew back, a question on his face. J.J. was being a good sport; I needed to be one, too, so I kissed him back deeply, passionately. I worked my issue, instead of letting it spoil things. J.J. was truly being a good sport about being shoved outside her comfort zone. It was just that her sportiness only required her to watch, not participate; my sportiness might be more, um, hands-on, and I was already one woman over my comfort limit, and it wasn't J.J.

I broke from the kiss, and was able to say with a normal voice, "I'm flattered."

"But part of why I'm here is that you already have a female lover and you're not very happy about it," J.J. said.

I turned enough in Nathaniel's arms to look at her. "Yeah."

"I've met Jade, she's beautiful."

"I've never argued that," I said.

"Besides you sharing memories of sex with women from the men in your life, which I admit is weird since you don't have those parts, what else bothers you about Jade?"

"I'd never thought of women as potential lovers before and suddenly I'm supposed to be the main lover of one; wouldn't that weird anyone out?"

J.J. nodded. "I'll give you that, but I can't help you with that. Is there anything specific that you're puzzled by? Anything about sex with another woman that you want to know from someone who's dated a lot of women?"

"A lot, huh?" Jason said.

She turned and gave him a big, mischievous smile. "You and I have exchanged our numbers; you know exactly how many women."

He laughed. "I knew we had a chance when your number was bigger than mine."

Knowing something about Jason's number of lovers, I was impressed, and a little . . . well, it's not everyone who hits triple digits for lovers. Once I would have been judgmental; now I was puzzled. Even with everyone I'd had in my life I was still under thirty lovers. I just couldn't imagine liking that many people that much.

Nathaniel held me close and whispered, "What do you want to know, Anita?"

I turned enough to look at him. "What do you mean?"

"What puzzles you the most about sex with another girl?"

I thought about it; hell, I'd been thinking about it. "One, the oral sex, it's so different in some ways, and Jade's still working through her issues with men so she won't let anyone but me and Domino go down on her, and I know I'm not doing it as well as I could, but I don't know what I'm doing wrong."

"Does she orgasm?" J.J. asked.

I fought free of a moment of embarrassment. "Eventually."

Nathaniel said, "Luckily Jade is fast clitorally."

"Jade let you watch?"

"Anita asked for some help with the oral, and hoped that I could give pointers through watching, and Jade agreed to it."

"And what did you learn?" J.J. asked.

"That Jade is one of those women who won't give feedback. I told Anita to ask, does this feel good, does that, but Jade won't give directions."

"Oh, God, I hate women like that," J.J. said.

"It's because her ex-master took all directions as criticism of his performance, and punished her for it," I said.

J.J.'s eyes went wide. "Well, that would teach anyone to keep their opinion to themselves."

"I understand where it comes from, why she doesn't help me, but it's like flying blind. I thought having the same parts would help, and it does a little. I can hear her breathing change, watch the little involuntary body movements, but I still think that if I could see someone else do it, and ask questions, maybe even trade off during so I could see actual demonstration, it would work much better."

"You are going at this in a very practical manner, Anita. I think I'm impressed, except are you treating it as a chore, not a pleasure?"

I fought not to squirm. "I go down on her because I know how much I love it, and she just started letting Domino try oral on her. She hasn't talked about it yet, but I suspect her old master didn't enjoy giving oral sex, so he made it unpleasant for her, like he made a lot of things unpleasant for her."

"Do you enjoy doing it?"

I sighed. "Not really; I don't get the high off it that I get from going down on men. Hell, I can orgasm sometimes from giving oral sex."

J.J. gave me wide eyes again. "Really?"

I nodded. "Really."

"Well, damn, I've heard that's possible, but I've never met anyone who could do it."

I fought not to be embarrassed again.

"Don't be embarrassed, Anita; it's great, amazing, no wonder you enjoy it so much."

"I enjoyed it before I started orgasming from it," I said, as if I wanted it clear it wasn't just about me having a happy. I don't know why, but somehow I felt defensive.

J.J. smiled as if she realized I was being defensive. "I feel the same way about going down on women, except I don't have an orgasm from it; be awesome if I did."

Jason laughed. "You'd never do anything else if you orgasmed from it."

She laughed, then sobered. "Not if it was just Freda."

I wondered if she knew she wasn't in love with her live-in girlfriend anymore. Was I supposed to say something about it, or let it go? I wasn't sure, so I let it go; one crisis at a time.

"Please tell me that I didn't ruin everything between you and Freda," Jason said, hugging her tighter.

"We had issues before you came back into my life, Jason. It's more like the more I enjoy spending time with you, the more I see that she and I don't have fun anymore."

"Love isn't always about fun," Nathaniel said.

"No, but shouldn't it be fun some of the time? I think I just hadn't realized how much Freda wants to change me into someone that I'm not, until Jason came along and just accepted me for who I really am."

"You accepted me, too," he said.

She smiled. "I did."

"I've never understood why people try to marry people that they want to change completely," I said.

"Me, either," she said. She looked at me, face serious, and then grinned.

"What?" I asked.

"Serious comment, but it sounds self-serving."

"Just tell me," I said.

"I would be happy to go down on Jade while you watched, and you could ask questions while I did it, but would she agree to it?"

"She and I talked about you before you got into town. She isn't afraid of women the way she is men. She is afraid of some female wereanimals, but not humans. Nothing personal but she doesn't see humans as much of a threat."

"No insult taken, it's just the truth. I've seen how fast Jason can move, and felt how strong he is, and no human can compete with it."

"Thanks, honeybunch," he said.

She smiled and stroked his arm. "You're welcome, sweetums." Then she looked back at me. "So Jade has agreed to sexual contact with me?"

"Yes, but she wanted it to be just the three of us and I wasn't comfortable with that; sorry to be all heterosexual nervous, but I need at least one guy in the bed."

"Really, you've never been alone with Jade?"

"No, and I feel bad about that, but after the foreplay I need boy parts, or it feels like it's not finished."

"Really?" J.J. said.

"Yep."

"Have you thought about strap-ons?"

"It's been brought up by some of the guys, but I don't really have interest in it, and I just can't wrap my head around Jade doing it to me."

"Why, because she's a girl?"

"No, honestly, because I see having someone use a strap-on as a dominant bondage thing, more than sex, and I don't bottom to women." That last was said in a tone that was very final. It was one of the few things I was sure of.

"I don't do a lot of bondage, but I don't see strap-ons as bondage."

"Po-tay-toe, po-tah-to," I said.

She nodded. "One person's sex is another person's kink, I get that."

"Also, Jade is so submissive that even if I had found a woman I was willing to let top me, it would never be her."

"Let me just say that a woman who's been abused like Jade can be tricky in bed even for someone like me, who's more experienced with women, and a lover who doesn't give feedback so you know if you're doing it right is really hard."

"So I'm not just being all stupid straight girl?"

Nathaniel hugged me. "I told you that you weren't."

"But you love me, and you're not a girl."

J.J. smiled. "No, you're not being all stupid straight girl. You're actually being very responsible and trying your best, which is a hell of a lot more than most lovers do."

"Thanks."

"You're welcome. I would be honored to try to help you do oral sex with Jade, but how different are you and Jade on oral sex?"

"What do you mean, different?"

"Nathaniel, you got to watch, how different are they?"

"From what I could see, Anita takes longer to go with oral, and in fact Jade can be incredibly quick clitorally if issues don't get in her way."

"Any other differences?"

"Jade's clit is lower down than Anita's, so the positioning is different, and I think that Jade likes less direct stimulation there than Anita, which makes Anita have to go even lower most of the time."

"That makes it harder to breathe sometimes if you bury your face deep; you could actually not be able to breathe." She looked at me, raising the gold arch of her eyebrows.

"Let me just say, this is all a little too clinical for me, and I'm very uncomfortable right now, but yeah, sometimes my ability to hold my breath, from doing boy oral, helps me go down on Jade, because it's just too weird to try to breathe and be that . . . low on her."

"Okay, that gives me a starting point," J.J. said, and then she grinned again, face lighting up with it.

"What?" I asked, and knew the one word sounded suspicious.

She rolled her eyes so she could glance at Jason,

and the look of mischief was so close to some of his, I knew I wasn't going to like whatever she was about to say.

"I know that look," Jason said. "Anita may not like what you're going to say."

"Should I not say it?"

He laughed. "Go ahead."

She turned back to me, face still shining with humor. "First, serious question: Would Jade let Jason be in the room?"

"I don't know; she hasn't before."

"What men does she allow?"

"Domino we actually have sex with; well, I have intercourse with him, but Jade doesn't yet. She lets him touch her and do her by hand and orally, so he's good. Nathaniel if he touches only me except for sleep cuddling, which was a big deal when she finally allowed it. Jean-Claude is okay, though she's still nervous around vampires, so he has to be careful of her issues."

"Does she have sex with Jean-Claude?"

"No."

"So Domino is the only man she lets touch her sexually at all?"

"Yes."

"Why just him?" she asked.

"I think it's because he's the only black tiger we have, and the clan tigers enjoy being with others of their own clan."

She mulled that over, and then said, "I wouldn't be comfortable having Domino, I don't know him. Jean-Claude makes me nervous in that cat-and-mouse sort of way. Nathaniel would be okay, but only if Jason was with us."

"I should have asked Jade about Jason, too. It was stupid of me not to take your nerves into account; I'm sorry."

"Don't be sorry, Anita; you're doing your best for Jade, for all of us." She seemed to think more on it, face very serious, eyes showing the level of concentration.

"I let them tie me up; Jade seems to like that," Nathaniel said.

"Nope," Jason said, "don't even ask. I don't bottom to submissives either, and I especially don't let myself get tied up with women who have serious issues with men."

"Jade's never hurt anyone," I said.

"No, but who knows what might send her into a flashback? Anita, she may seem all gentle with you, but when she's working out in the gym she's wicked fast and stronger than that body looks; if she could get over the issues her old master beat into her she would be one of the most efficient killing machines I've ever seen."

I blinked at him. "Jade?"

"She doesn't work out in front of you to the best of her ability, Anita. I think that goes back to her old master not liking that maybe she was faster or better at some of the fighting skills than he was; I think she doesn't want to show you up."

"She's a weretiger, Jason; she's supposed to be faster and stronger than I am."

"You know that, but she sure as hell isn't comfortable with you seeing her in the gym. Haven't you noticed that she never works out when you're there unless forced?"

I thought about it, and then said, "Is that why she sucks at hand to hand and most weapons practice, because I'm always there?"

"I think so, because when you're not in the weight room, or the track, or . . . she works a heavy bag over like she'd make a person into so much meat, real quick."

"Have you seen her do that?" I asked Nathaniel.

"Yes, but only when you and Nicky aren't with me. She's different without the two of you in the gym."

"Okay, I sort of understand her having issues with showing me up, but why does she care about Nicky?"

"I think she doesn't want anyone she considers a threat to see how good she is," Jason said.

"Nicky hasn't threatened her, has he?" I asked.

"No, he hasn't hurt her; he's just really big, really physical, and really good at fighting."

"Well, crap," I said.

"I wouldn't let anyone tie me down and put me

at her mercy; just call me cautious, but there's a look in her eyes sometimes that I do not want aimed at me when I can't fight back," Jason said.

"You're not a fighter," I said.

"I'm not a bodyguard, but I'm a werewolf, and that means you have to fight to keep your place in the pack. All wereanimals can fight, Anita, but I also know I'm a small guy. That limits me."

"Micah is smaller than you and he's an alpha."

"Yeah, but he's way more ruthless than I am. He's more like you. You'll both just kill people if they threaten you or your people. I won't go for the kill unless I have to; that makes me not a threat."

J.J. looked from one to the other of us. "Are you serious about the killing part?"

Jason and I exchanged a look. I don't know what we would have said, because Nathaniel said, "I think that look in Jade's eyes is why I liked being tied up with her in the bed."

That made us all look at him, which was probably what he'd planned. He was distracting J.J. from the fact that she could know most of our sex secrets, but the violence part . . . she was too much a civilian to know that part.

"You know that Jade is dangerous, so it gives you a kick to be tied up and at her mercy?" I asked.

He nodded. "Asher thinks she's the perfect victim and would love to have her in the dungeon, but I think he's wrong. I think that under the right circumstances, Jade would be incredibly dangerous." He gave a little cuddling shiver, and I felt his body begin to react where it had been pressed inert against the back of my body. The thought of how dangerous she might be excited him. I loved Nathaniel more than almost anyone, but there were moments, like this, when I didn't understand him. I liked the pretend of danger in bondage with people I trusted utterly; yes, I pushed the edge, but not like Nathaniel did. He liked real danger when he could get it, and thanks to being a wereleopard, he healed almost anything, emphasis on the "almost."

"And you like that?" Jason said.

"You know I do," Nathaniel said.

Jason shook his head. "Raina cured me of ever

letting another wereanimal tie me down and have their way with me."

I felt stupid and slow; I'd forgotten how Jason became a werewolf. Raina, the now-dead alpha female of the local pack, their lupa, had tied him up, had sex with him, and shifted to wolf-woman form on top of him, and he'd been fine with that, but then she'd used claws and teeth on him. I'd shared that memory thanks to Raina's ghost, and I knew that she hadn't cared if Jason lived or died. It had all been about her pleasure in that moment. She'd been a true sexual sadist, and where she had no conscience a pure sociopath, but like most sociopaths I knew, there were places where she cared; she just never seemed to give a damn for her lovers.

"Raina went farther than even I wanted to go," Nathaniel said, and he held me closer. I remembered him telling me that she'd done what would have amounted to a snuff film if he'd been human. He'd agreed to what she did, but hadn't understood that some fantasies are never, ever meant to be real—not if you want to live and stay sane.

"I'm sorry, Jason, I forgot how you became a werewolf. Will watching Nathaniel be tied up while Jade plays with him be like a triggering event for the memory?" I asked.

J.J. hugged his arms tighter around her. "I still can't believe that she did that to you. She was like a serial killer."

I gave points to both of them that Jason had shared the story with J.J. and that she had been sympathetic and not blamed the victim for the kinky sex.

Jason looked at Nathaniel. "Doesn't it bother you to be tied up and at the mercy of another female wereanimal, after what I know she did to you, too?"

"I enjoyed most of what she did more than you did. I still miss Gabriel and her sometimes."

Jason shuddered and held J.J. tighter. "I don't miss either of them."

If J.J. hadn't been in the room I would have said, *And I don't regret killing either of them*, but I didn't want to bring up the killing thing again. The police actually knew that I'd killed them in self-defense after they'd kidnapped me and tried to make me star

147

in one of Raina's real-life snuff films. They'd also tried to kill Jean-Claude and Richard off camera. No, I had no regrets about their deaths, nope, none. My conscience was so clean on that one that it was shiny.

"I like being tied up for Anita and Jade, and it's helping her gain more confidence," Nathaniel said.

"Would you let Jade tie you up, just you and her?" Jason asked.

"She wouldn't want that, to be alone with just me, but no, I wouldn't."

"You think she'd really hurt you if I wasn't there?" I asked.

"I don't believe that Jade would ever hurt me, not really, but the men she sees as a threat, if they stepped over the line, she might kill first and ask your forgiveness later."

"Agreed," Jason said.

I looked from one to the other of them. "How did I miss this?"

"Jade wanted you to miss it," Jason said.

"Is she dangerous to me?" J.J. asked.

He hugged and kissed her. "No, if I thought she was I wouldn't have brought you here."

"I'd still rather have you in the room with us, just in case," she said.

"Me, too," he said.

"Who gets to negotiate with Jade about extra men in the room?" I asked.

Everyone looked at me. "Why me?" I said, and even to me it sounded whiny.

"You're her master," Jason said.

"You rescued her from hundreds of years of torment; it makes her trust you above everyone," Nathaniel said.

Both excellent points, so I went off to negotiate with a beautiful weretiger about bringing another woman into our bed for a girly three-way, and oh, by the way, I was throwing in Nathaniel, Jason, and honestly if I could manage it, Domino. I wasn't sure how J.J. would feel about that last addition, but I'd try for it, for my own comfort level. I wasn't homophobic, but I was confused about women. I'd always thought being a lesbian must be easier, because you were a girl dating girls, so you had a leg up on understanding each other. Nope, didn't work that way, not at all. Dating a woman wasn't that much different from dating men, except I sort of understood how to date men. Women confused me, or this woman did. She was like a field of emotional land mines that I didn't know how to avoid. Were all women like this? Was this how my men felt about me? God, I hoped not.

7

JADE WANTED TO try oral sex with J.J. and me, but she didn't see the need for any men joining us. I stood firm. She cried, told me I didn't love her. I let the emotional storm wash over. When I didn't give in, she did. So I would spend J.J.'s second night in St. Louis with the most women I'd ever voluntarily allowed in a bed with me. Jinkies.

Jean-Claude gave us permission to use the big bed in his bedroom. We'd coined the term "orgy-sized" for the custom-made bed. It was a heavy four-poster with attachment points here and there for chains and rope.

It was really the only bed big enough to hold everybody, if by some miracle J.J. and Jade both got comfortable enough to allow everyone on the bed. That was a big *if*, but I planned my sex like I planned my vampire hunts. Plan for every eventuality: It keeps you alive when chasing rogue vampires, and it keeps your relationships alive after the big bondage sex scene.

The bedspread, bed drapes, and pillows all changed periodically. Today the bedspread was white with black and red pillows piled at the headboard, and curtains of red and black with white gauze in between. There was even a coverlet at the foot of the bed in red and black with a center flower of white. I'd thought it was a dogwood blossom when I first saw it, but it was a stylized rose, I was told. It was beautiful, whatever it was supposed to be.

I sat in the mounded pillows with Jade curled beside me. We were sitting above the ropes that held Nathaniel spread-eagled on the bed. Yes, the bed was that big, so that there was still room between the ropes that held his arms for the two of us to sit together and not touch the bindings, or Nathaniel's arms. When he'd been tied in place, I'd watched his eyes, saw the peacefulness that filled them just by being bound, "helpless." The rope was woven hemp dyed black, very stark against the white bedspread. He was the only one who was nude yet, that beautiful body spread and held on the bed, waiting for what we'd negotiated. We'd undone his ankle-length auburn hair and spread it out like a silken pool underneath and around his body like a red and chestnut halo; it looked more red than normal against the white of the cover. We probably should have taken the bedspread off and gotten to sheets before we tied him in place, because the chances were good we'd ruin the white cover before the night was over; some things even a good dry cleaner can't clean off.

Jade was wearing a red silk nightie that was almost identical to the second blue one that J.J. was wearing. Apparently she liked blue lingerie. I'd changed to a black one myself; the teddy had been a little too see-through for the night as planned. I'd agreed to have sex, so the lingerie would be disappearing at some point and there'd be a lot of naked going on, so it seemed a little silly to not want to wear something sheer to start with, but sometimes it's not about logic, it's about feeling comfortable in the moment. I needed all the comfort I could get tonight.

Jade's hair fell to her waist like shining black water, startling against the scarlet of her lingerie. It clung over her small, tight breasts and the cool air made the nipples stand out starkly against the cloth. She was already holding my hand. Her nail polish was black, mine was red; we both had lipstick as red as the silk on her and in the pillows behind us, so that we looked like we'd matched everything on purpose. Her large, uptilted eyes were the color of orange and yellow fire. It was the mark of the black tiger clan to have flame-colored eyes. The red of the silk brought out the red hidden in her eyes, so that they looked utterly inhuman and amazing with the eyeliner like a black frame around all that color. I admit that I tried to see that look in her eyes that Jason and Nathaniel had talked about, which frightened one of them and excited the other, but she looked as she always looked to me, like a beautiful victim.

She was shorter than I was, more petite, so that when we stood she fitted under my arm like I did with most of the men in my life.

I ran my thumb over her knuckles over and over, to reassure us both. She liked to touch me, in some ways needed to touch me, but she was usually still when we touched, holding on, but not petting until sex started. I'd asked her about it once and been informed that her ex-master had liked her to hold on, but not to pet him, and I knew the kinds of things he'd done to teach her his rules. I'd broken her ties with him metaphysically, and my one regret was that I hadn't hunted him down and killed him yet. We had other people hunting him now. I'd learned that when you're king you can't always go slaying the dragons, because if the king dies the kingdom needs a new king, and the next one may be a real bastard. I risked myself enough as a U.S. Marshal; I wasn't allowed vendettas.

I stayed with Jade and kept her safe; that was my job. Hunting down her tormentor and killing his ass was left to guards who were also ancient vampires and knew him of old.

J.J. stood beside the bed holding Jason's hand. "If I clapped my hands and made happy bat noises, would anyone get mad at me?" she asked.

He shook his head. "I wouldn't, I'm just sad I'm only allowed to watch. I'm more exhibitionist than voyeur."

She kissed his cheek. "I'm sorry, honeybunch."

"I feel your pain," Domino said from the other side of the bed.

J.J. had agreed that he could strip down to a pair of silken boxers similar to what Jason was wearing. It was fair in case either she or Jade relented and let me have my extra guy in the bed, or let each other have their lover. Jason's silk was a blue that almost matched J.J.'s nightie; Domino's was a red that matched Jade's, since I'd bought both his and hers as a pair. Jean-Claude had helped me pick the color so that it was a perfect match of scarlets.

"I know you do, bro," Jason said, and gave a fist bump to the air that Domino returned in the air on his side of the bed. I'd have traded places with either of them in a hot minute, so that I didn't have to do this particular scene. In a way Jade topped from the bottom, which was a phrase to describe the way a submissive could control a relationship even though the dominant was supposed to be the one in control.

Technically, I should have been able to dictate to her that I wanted Jason in the bed, and she'd just have to deal, but the submissive had a full vote, and she'd said no. I had a full vote, too, and could have said, *Jason is in the bed or we're done*, but I hadn't. Why hadn't I? Because I wasn't sure whether I really wanted him in the bed with me as much as I just didn't want J.J. and Jade there, and that was the truth. I was so far outside my comfort zone I couldn't see it from the shore anymore. I felt lost at sea, but determined to weather the storm, even if it was a storm formed of soft flesh and silk. To do anything else would be cowardice, and I couldn't do that, wouldn't do that. I wouldn't be a coward on something so important to this many people I valued, loved. This was too important for my issues to win. Either you work your issues, or they will work you. It wasn't so much Jade topping from the bottom, it was me, my near-panic driving me forward and forcing me to face whatever the hell bothered me about extra women in the bed with me.

I sat there rubbing my thumb faster and faster across Jade's knuckles as if her hand were a worry stone, and if I just petted hard enough I'd figure out what was wrong in my head to make me this uncomfortable.

I had female friends who were this afraid of multiple men in bed, as if more men equaled rape, but for me, men were like a security blanket. Women scared me, and I had no idea why. I just knew that I wouldn't let this fear best me any more than I let fear of that noise in the dark keep me from going in gun ready, searching for the rogue vampire I knew was inside. All fear is the same no matter the cause of it; you conquer or are conquered by it. I wasn't into losing, not even to myself, maybe especially to myself.

I told myself I could safe-word at any moment, and kept trying to rub a hole through Jade's hand.

Jade leaned in and whispered, "Are you all right, Anita?"

Truth was, no, but out loud I said, "Sure."

She gave me a look, and if we'd lowered our metaphysical shielding, she could have felt everything I was feeling, and I her, just like I could do with Domino, Jason, and Nathaniel. Jade was my black tiger to call, Domino was my white/black, Jason my wolf, and Nathaniel my leopard to call. They were my animals to call, my *Moítié Bête*; we all had to work at not sensing each other's emotions.

Of course the tension singing down my hand into Jade's probably gave me away just fine. You don't have to be psychic to pick up on the obvious.

"Anita," Jason said.

I looked at him and J.J.

"You okay?"

I shrugged. "I think this is the most complicated BDSM scene I've tried without Jean-Claude or Asher involved. It's like we have all this talent and potential, but no one is in charge." That was all true. It wasn't exactly what was spooking me, but it was still part of the truth. It also meant that they'd probably quit asking me what was wrong.

"I cannot be with Asher," Jade said.

I shook my head. "I wasn't suggesting it, just not sure who's directing everything."

"We've made love with Nathaniel in bed with us before," she said, her voice soft, low, and strangely musical. Her voice didn't always sound that way, but it often did when she was trying to persuade, or I guess manipulate me. I'd asked her if she'd had theater training, but she didn't seem to know what I meant, so I'd let it go. I let a lot of things go with Jade, even I knew that, but when she puzzled me enough I stepped back rather than pushing. I wasn't sure if I was growing up, or she was winning.

"You're in charge, Anita," Domino said, "so be in charge. What do you want to do?"

In my head I thought, *Leave*. Maybe it showed on my face, because he said, "Do what you enjoy and Jade will follow your lead."

Jade nodded.

"Really?" I asked her.

"Truly," she said.

"Okay, I know what I want to do."

"I will follow where you lead," she said.

I knew it was both the truth and a lie. She'd follow me for a while, until she decided she didn't want to, or she got too uncomfortable, then she'd do whatever the hell she wanted to do and somehow it would be my fault, again. I was starting to seriously sympathize with the men who were dating me.

8

I SNUGGLED DOWN against the left side of Nathaniel's bound body, and Jade mirrored me on his right. I started by kissing those full lips of his; he kissed me back with his eyes already losing their focus as he began to give himself over to the rope, to our touch, to simply not being in control. It was one of my favorite things about bondage.

Jade leaned over, but didn't kiss him; she offered her red lips to me. She had never kissed Nathaniel on the mouth. It was something she saved for me. We kissed and it was a mingling of identical scarlet lipstick. She'd started wearing my shade of red, because if she wore something else it ruined both our lipsticks, or made colors that looked good on neither of us. I realized that she got more kisses now that our lipsticks matched; good thing the color looked good on both of us.

Nathaniel watched us kiss, his lips touched with red just down the center. He'd coined it the go-faster stripe, and wore it proudly. There was an eagerness in his eyes that wasn't just the submission; he liked seeing us kiss above him. I loved it when he and Micah kissed, so I totally got that he liked seeing me kiss another woman. Funny, I hadn't thought he had that typical male fantasy of two women and him; just goes to prove that bisexual doesn't mean not guy, just a different kind of guy.

I kissed him again, leaving our mingled reds brighter on his lips, and then moved to the warm sweetness of his neck, breathing in the vanilla scent of him, before laying a perfect red lip print against his skin. Jade mirrored me on the other side of his neck. I kissed the top of his shoulder, then the very beginning of his chest, feeling the flex of his muscles as he pulled at the rope that bound that arm. Nathaniel and I both liked to test our bonds, not to get away, but more to feel the pull and know we were trapped, held, helpless, at the same time that we knew we were not. All he had to do was say his safeword and I'd untie him. The same held true when it was my turn to be tied up. Bondage was the illusion of danger, not the real thing. I'd been tied up for real by bad guys and that wasn't exciting at all, just scary.

I laid my mouth over the mound of his pectoral muscle just above his nipple, and Jade kissed him at almost the same time so that we were beginning to truly mirror each other across Nathaniel's body. I put my mouth over his nipple and licked just the tip of my tongue across him, back and forth, quick strokes until his nipple became a small, firm point. I rolled my eyes upward so that I could look across his body at Jade, and found her fire-colored eyes looking at me. I used my tongue to lick and tease his nipple, keeping my eye contact all for Jade. Nathaniel began to make soft, eager noises for us.

We kissed slowly down his body an inch at a time, marked in red lipstick prints across his skin. We placed the last kiss on the top of his foot, just below the black circle of rope around his ankles.

I sat back, kneeling to look at our handiwork. There was something incredibly satisfying seeing him stretched beautiful and nude with the tracks of our lip prints decorating all that bare skin. His groin was untouched, but we'd both planted kisses all around it on his thighs and hips, until he'd whimpered. His body was more than ready to be touched, straight, hard, and eager. I'd avoided the area partially to up the teasing, but mostly because Jade was mirroring my lead better than she ever had before with Nathaniel and I wanted her to keep doing that. She'd already let me push her outside her usual comfort zone; I wanted to ease her further out, not push her off the cliff, not yet.

It wasn't just kindness, or even caution on my part. Jason and J.J. stood by the bed doing their own light petting. I knew that she was waiting for me to say, *Okay, come aboard*. There were so many possibilities of cliffs tonight that I didn't want to be pushed off either, so I wouldn't push Jade. Treat people as you want to be treated, and hopefully that whole karma thing works out.

Touching Nathaniel had helped me gather myself—*grounding and centering*, my friend and teacher Marianne would have called it. Whatever you called it, I felt better, more sure of myself and everything else, including the people around me.

I crawled over Nathaniel's legs and went to Jade. I wrapped her in my arms, drew her in close and kissed her, not just so she wouldn't get mad at me, but because I wanted to. She was mine, and she'd been very brave and marvelously sensual with Nathaniel. I kissed her, tongue sliding inside her mouth, my eager hands sliding over the silk she was wearing. I thought, as I thought almost every time I French-kissed her, that women had smaller mouths than men. She was so tiny in my hands, delicate bones and flesh, that she triggered the instinct that you should protect that which is smaller than you are. In reality she could have overturned a small car without breaking a sweat, but in that moment I kissed my delicate girl, feeling protective and proud, and drew back from the kiss leaving her breathing hard, her pupils huge with the endorphin rush of my attentions.

We'd smeared our lipstick, but not that much. I'd learned to kiss without ending up looking like a clown from kissing the men; now it was just a slightly more delicate dance with two women, two lipsticked mouths. Jade and I were learning. Of course, tonight if we didn't smear our lipsticks all to hell, we'd be doing it wrong.

I turned and looked at Jason and J.J. They were still holding each other, but had stopped making out to watch. I didn't know when they'd gone fully voyeur on the show, when Jade and I were still kissing our way down Nathaniel, or when I kissed Jade. Didn't know, didn't care; all I cared about was that as I crawled across the bed toward them, J.J. watched me like a bird that sees the snake coming, fascinated and a little afraid, as if she thought I might eat her, which was sort of funny since I was the only other non-wereanimal in the room. But there are all kinds of ways to be devoured; taking actual flesh is just one of them.

I crawled to the very edge of the bed and held my hand out to her. "I want your lipstick smeared all over ours."

J.J. hugged Jason tighter and said, "She moves like you do sometimes, like she has more muscles and tendons than humans have, dangerous sexy graceful."

I laughed then. "If you think I'm the most graceful thing on this bed, you are so wrong."

She smiled then, gave Jason a quick kiss, and took my hand, and I pulled her onto the bed.

9

I STARTED THE kiss with J.J., but there was no hesitation from her; she fell into the kiss with eager hands and mouth. She definitely kissed back, much more aggressive than Jade usually was. I stiffened for a second, debating how I felt, and then I gave back eagerness for eagerness and let my hands knead her body underneath the blue silk. My hands expected softness, and found some of the leanest muscle stretched over the most delicate body I'd ever held, so she felt both fragile and incredibly strong at the same time. Jade might have been an amazing athlete when I wasn't looking, but her body still felt soft and you had to search for the muscles. J.J.'s strength was right there at the surface, covered in warm, smooth skin.

Her pink lipstick was smeared with my red, and I knew my lipstick must look as bad. It wasn't neat, but it didn't look like clown makeup either, it looked . . . like we'd smeared it kissing each other wildly. But wait . . . we had.

It made me laugh almost wildly. J.J. gave me a questioning look out of her clear blue eyes, and I reached for her again, sliding my hands underneath the bit of blue silk, so that I could feel more of that taut, satin-kissed, muscled skin. I realized vaguely that I was getting an echo of someone in my head and it wasn't me. I wasn't being invaded by some evil spirit, but I shared memories with Jean-Claude, and he had loved women for more centuries than America had been a country. Somewhere in his past had been someone that J.J. reminded him of, and I was able to get that fierce, happy echo without having to experience the actual memory. I liked that.

But I'd also had to own that if I hadn't agreed with

the joyful eagerness of Jean-Claude's memory, it couldn't have forced me to do anything I didn't want to do. I wanted to slide the blue silk over J.J.'s head and see the body I'd been touching, so that I saw the blue lace of her thong sitting against the lean swell of her hips. I wanted to run my hands over all that lean and feminine muscle, so I did. Her breasts were so small and she so lean that they were almost just an extension of the pectoral muscle like men can get, but when I cupped them in my hands they were soft, moving and changing as I squeezed and caressed them. To get as much breast in my hand as I wanted I had to mound one up, so that I could lean over and wrap my mouth tight around her, and suck. I did it until she cried out, "God!" It encouraged me a little too much, so that she had to say, "Too hard, less teeth."

I eased up, and pulled back to find our mingled lipsticks decorating her breast as if I'd painted it with my mouth. Some movement caught my eye and I found Jason holding on to one of the dark wooden bedposts. His fingers were holding on to the heavy carving of the bed like it was an anchor to hold him where he was, and his face was more than eager. His eyes held something close to pain, and I remembered that he, like me, wasn't much of a watcher. We were both more doers.

I turned and looked at Nathaniel, still tied in the middle of the big bed, unable to come play. His lavender eyes were some of the darkest purple I'd ever seen them, lips half parted, face raw with lust. His body was eager and ready just from watching me with the other women. He didn't have this reaction to just Jade and me, and I realized that he liked J.J.'s less complicated eagerness, too.

Domino had moved to the bed, his fingers actually touching the edge of it. He was fighting to keep his face neutral and failing, but he was trying. Nathaniel wasn't hiding how he felt, but then he was nude and male, it was a little late to hide. Domino controlled his face, but his body was so hard and tight against the red silk undies that it made me want to crawl over there and touch him, strip him of the silk and have him join us.

I turned last to Jade, because only she had moved farther away from us; all the men who could move closer, had. Her face was very careful, trying for neutral, but I knew the set of her shoulders, that almost hunched look. I realized in that moment that I'd have done better, had fewer issues, if she were more dominant a personality, had more aggression and surety to throw in with mine, rather than making me chase, seduce, when I didn't truly want to do either.

J.J.'s hands slid under my own bit of black silk, and there was a demand to her touch, a lack of tentativeness that I liked a lot. Maybe my biggest trouble with Jade wasn't that she was female, but that she was so uncertain, so that I always had to persuade, do all the planning, and just court her in a way that the men normally courted me. As J.J. pushed me back against the bed I had a feeling that she wouldn't make me be in charge of all the relationship. Yay, so yay!

What do you do in the middle of making out with one woman, when you realize your other lover may not be the girl of your dreams? You reach for her, because you can't bear to see that careful sadness on her face, so I did. She rewarded me with one of the most brilliant smiles I'd ever seen on her face, and I couldn't do anything but smile back, and then J.J.

worked my nightie up over my breasts and pressed her mouth to one of them, and the smiling turned into me making wordless, eager noises for her.

Jade pulled her red silk over her head and threw it behind her. She bent over me, kissing me upside down, while J.J. tried to put as much of my breast into her mouth as she could. It might have made me giggle, except that Jade's mouth was pressed to mine, the silk of her hair falling around my face.

J.J. began to suck on my breast and I didn't feel like giggling anymore. Jade leaned over me, her breasts brushing my face as she bent over my other breast and licked over my nipple. I mounded her breast in my hand and returned the favor. Her body shivered for me, and then she used her hand to draw my breast up, so she could suck on my nipple, and all three of us began to suck, lick, and nibble a breast apiece. We had three leftover breasts and more mouths in the room. I would have loved to bring Jason and Domino onto the bed to join the breast play, and the thought of Nathaniel only being able to watch it all tightened things low in my body, not because I wanted to exclude him, but because I knew how much it would excite him to be forced to only watch with his body so eager to join. But what works in fantasy doesn't always work in reality; if you add too many people it can go from erotic and exciting to a game of Jenga. Adding the boys, even if both women would have agreed, might have been too much, like Internet porn: sex that no one really enjoys, but it looks impressive, and gives you bragging rights of *I'm kinkier than thou.*

I bit a little harder on Jade's breast, and she startled. The reaction let me know it was too hard for her. I was beginning to suspect that I'd bite breasts harder if I could find a woman who enjoyed it.

J.J. raised her mouth up enough to ask, "Do you like breast play as hard as you like other things?"

I had to let go of Jade's breast to answer, "Yes."

J.J. looked back at Jason. "How hard can I bite?"

He answered still holding on to the bedpost. His voice sounded much calmer than the look in his eyes. "Bite down with slowly increasing pressure; Anita will let you know when you've reached her limit."

J.J. turned back to me with wide eyes. "Really?"

"Yes," Domino answered, from the edge of the bed where he had wrapped his arms around himself, as if he were holding himself back from the bed with his own physical force.

A shiver of power made me look at Nathaniel, who was only a couple of feet from us. His eyes had bled to the rich gray-blue of his leopard's eyes. He was the only blue-eyed leopard I'd ever seen, as if even in animal form his eyes had to be unusual.

J.J. used her hand to mound my breast up so that she could slide her mouth over it, and then she began to bite down slowly, so that it was just pressure.

"Harder," I said.

She rolled her eyes up, and they were uncertain, but she put more pressure, and after two more times of me saying, "Harder," she was in the ballpark for how hard I wanted it in that moment. Some nights I didn't want to be bitten, but tonight was not one of those nights.

I breathed out, "Harder!"

Her eyes rolled up to me and finally held that darkness I had never seen in another woman, like the eyes of a lioness looking over the body of a gazelle, and she bit me. It bowed my spine, threw me writhing over the bedspread, hands grabbing at the bedspread for something, anything, to hold on to. I found Jade's hand, but she pulled away so that I was left with the bedcovers wrapped in my hands while J.J.'s mouth rode my breast.

I cried out for her, and finally said, "Safeword, safeword, stop, stop!"

She rose up from my breast and left a red ring of her teeth imprinted on my right breast. She hadn't bled me, but it was a nice mark.

"Did I hurt you?" she asked, voice breathy and a little thick.

"No," I said, and laughed, "no."

She moved up so she was even with me, and studied my face for a moment, and then she smiled. "That was fun."

"Yes, yes it was," I said, and my voice was breathless and happy.

Some small sound made me turn my head. Domino had moved farther away from the bed; Nathaniel had his eyes closed, body straining against the ropes, as he fought for his own control. It was Jade kneeling in the pillows at the head of the bed, tears shining on her face.

I sighed, and lay there for a second, not wanting to go to her, because there had been other times with Domino, or Nathaniel, where I'd gotten some of the rougher foreplay that I liked, and Jade had freaked. She had so many triggers that reminded her of her abusive ex-master, and most of those triggers tended to be sex that I enjoyed.

J.J. looked down at me, and I didn't try to hide the look in my eyes. "Sorry," I said.

"It's okay, not your fault."

"No," I said, "it isn't." I got up so I could go and comfort the other woman in the bed, but honestly, I didn't want to. It wasn't that I was unsympathetic. It was that I'd been sympathetic for months and months. She wouldn't go to therapy unless I went with her, and I'd told her, no, therapy was an inner journey and had to be walked alone, and besides, you weren't honest if other people were in the room. I'd finally found a therapist who specialized in domestic abuse survivors, and I'd gone with her, but she had made it all about how we weren't getting along, so it turned into couples counseling. I'd tried to bring up the abuse she'd suffered from her ex-master, and all Jade had wanted to talk about was how to make her and me a better, more workable couple. I finally told the counselor that since I was already engaged to three men, I didn't really see how a girlfriend who didn't like men that much was going to fit into my life. It's not often you see a really good psychiatrist stumped, but she didn't have a comeback for that.

Jade had cried and tried to get me to go back to the counselor with her, but I had stood firm, so since I wouldn't go and hold her hand, she wouldn't see the counselor. Jade wasn't ready to deal with her past. She was so broken, but that wasn't the problem; Nathaniel had been broken when I met him. The difference was that Nathaniel had been willing to work his shit, to try to get better, but Jade wouldn't help herself get better. She just wanted to cling to me, and to Domino to a much lesser extent, and be afraid. If I'd been in love with her I'd have been more patient, but I so wasn't in love with her, as I crawled over the bed to dry her tears. I fought to keep my feelings off my face.

Nathaniel made a small sound as I crawled even with his face. I looked down at him, and he whispered, "Love you."

"Love you more."

"Love you mostest," he said.

I smiled and leaned over for a kiss. His lips tasted and felt so right. I was surprised when I drew back that there was lipstick on his mouth, faintly, but there. I'd have thought it had all been worn away by now.

I stroked his hair, the side of his face, so that he leaned his face into my hand like a cat will, to rub against your skin and mark you as theirs, and I was his, so much his. But I was also Jade's, or she wanted me to be. I looked at her huddled against the headboard, crying, and left my wonderful boy for later, after I'd handled the crisis at hand.

My breast ached as I moved over the bed; just the movement of the breast itself made it hurt more, and it was a wonderful reminder of J.J.'s mouth on my body. I liked the pain as I crawled over the bed, but the happy endorphins were fading as I let Jade wrap herself around me. It took everything I had not to recoil away from her, or be angry at her. I'd talked to my own counselor about Jade, but could only talk about my issues with the situation. Jade wouldn't talk to anyone about herself, except me and a few others here, like Envy, but we were her friends, her lovers, and the damage she was suffering from was above our pay grade. This was professional-level broken, and none of us were professionals at fixing it.

J.J. came and helped me comfort Jade. J.J. was able to talk and soothe better than I could, because she didn't have the emotional baggage I was fighting through, so the two of us got her calmed down. I probably would have given in and done the sex just the way Jade wanted it, though honestly, it didn't appeal to me, but J.J. helped us come to a compromise.

We used Nathaniel's body for the "pillow" to prop Jade up high enough for oral sex. She put her red silk nightie back on, but it was actually very brave of her to be willing to lay her nearly naked lower body across his groin. On the other hand, she was getting oral sex from not one but two women—like I said, a compromise.

Jade was only comfortable with her bits pointing toward Domino's side of the bed, but J.J. was naked, too, so I thought there'd be a problem from her about Domino seeing her, but there wasn't.

She said, "I dance nearly nude sometimes; you deal with the issue, or it hurts your performance." She said it in a tone that made it clear that she didn't let anything mess with her performance.

So, J.J. lay on the bed with the back of her naked body pointed to Domino's side of the bed; if it bothered her that a strange man was getting to see her most intimate parts, you couldn't tell it. I liked that a lot.

In fact, J.J. wrapped her hands around Jade's thighs, and buried her face between her legs with a practiced comfort that I envied. I wasn't sure I'd ever be that comfortable with another woman. So many men in my life had been such good sports about sharing me with other men, or even interacting with the other men, that I felt it was almost a failing on my part not to be as good a sport myself. If that sounds weird, then so be it; it was how I felt.

Nathaniel lay on the bed, pressed to the white satin bedspread, his hair shining against the white like a red-brown pool, outlining his body and theirs like auburn lace edging some kinky valentine. J.J. lay on the edge of his hair, her nude body like a work of art carved in muscle and the bare swell of hips through her own art. I realized that she had sculpted her body as carefully, with as much love and passion, as any piece of marble had ever been carved by chisel and hand. Her blond hair fell like yellow water around her shoulders, hiding most of Jade's lower body from the room. Jade lay on top of Nathaniel, most of her body covered by the startling scarlet of the silk, her long black hair spread out behind her turned to the color of raven's wings and night skies by the white of the bedspread, and the pillow we'd propped under her head, and the red contrast of her clothes, and her own pale skin. None of them were tanned, but with their bodies pressed so close together you could see that Nathaniel was naturally darker. Jade was second palest, with white skin that hadn't seen the touch of the sun in most of the last few centuries, so that her black hair and fire-colored eyes were all the more shocking, and then J.J. with her milk-white skin to match the yellow hair and the spring-blue eyes. In fact, her hair hid most of what she was doing. I could tell she was doing different things from Jade's reaction, but could see precious little of the action even kneeling beside them all.

I knew progress was happening, because Jade's breathing was speeding up, and her eyes were starting to soft-focus. Nathaniel's arms and legs were straining in the ropes, his eyes fluttering shut, and I realized for the first time that having a silk-clad woman writhing on his groin while another woman ate her out might actually bring him. We hadn't planned on that, because usually his stamina and control were phenomenal, but this was a new type of scene for him, and new sometimes flipped your switch quicker than you'd planned.

I was torn between trying to watch what J.J. was doing so I might learn something, and asking

Nathaniel how close he was, and finally moved close enough to stroke his cheek and make him look at me. His eyes had bled back to lavender from their earlier leopard, but they were still soft-focused, and he had to fight to narrow his vision on my face.

"Are you close?"

He shook his head, but then his neck bowed, eyes closing. His arms strained against the ropes, his body quivering with sensations. I looked back at the other women. Jade looked like she was doing a crunch push-up, her face showing something between pain and utter pleasure. I watched her body writhe, while all she was feeling crossed her face, soundlessly. She almost never cried out during oral, I wasn't sure why, but it meant that her body reacting was often my only clue that I'd hit the right combination.

Nathaniel managed to say, "No, not close."

Domino's voice came from behind us. "Why in the name of God not?"

"I'm with Domino on this one," Jason said; he'd moved to the bedpost on this corner so he had a view from the side, rather than staring at the women's heads.

J.J. raised her head up, and her mouth and chin shone in the lamplight. "I hadn't thought about Nathaniel going from this; can he take more, or do we need to move her?"

"No moving," Jade said, in a voice that was thick with the screams she never let herself have.

"Don't move," Nathaniel said; his tone was distracted, but his words were clear.

"Okay, then," J.J. said, and turned to look at me. "Did you see anything I did?"

I shook my head. "Not really."

"Then come down here where you can see."

"Yes, ma'am," I said, hesitated, and then thought, *How else am I going to learn?* Screw it; we'd make it a tutorial.

10

I GOT DOWN beside J.J. so I could watch more closely. I was vaguely aware that Jason and Domino were both behind us, still not on the bed, but getting the best view they could. I didn't care, they were both my lovers, they'd seen me before. They were both seeing one new naked lady apiece, but even Jade had stopped caring about that; something about the second orgasm had helped her get over her insecurities about Jason seeing her nude for the first time.

"Wait, what did you do just now to make her body react like that?" I asked.

J.J. rose back from the other woman's body enough to say, "I licked here along the edge instead of down the center. She doesn't seem to like a lot of direct clitoral contact until she's closer to going."

"How can you tell she's ready for more direct contact?"

"Breathing quickens, and she clenches her hands; it's like a tell in poker."

"So everyone's tell is different," I said.

"Sort of; almost every woman's breath speeds up, and her face reacts in some way, unless the orgasm catches her by surprise."

I nodded. "I do that sometimes, so I get that."

"You want a turn?" she asked.

"Yeah, that way if I'm not getting the same reactions you can help answer questions."

"It's like a lesbian tutorial," Jason said.

We both turned and gave him a look over our shoulders. He held his hands out, like no harm meant, but honestly it might have been a record for the longest he'd ever gone without making a joke of some kind.

"Maybe you'll learn a few things, too," J.J. said.

"Are you saying I need to learn?" he asked.

She grinned. "Well, no, you're excellent, but still, it's not just a lesbian skill."

Domino raised his hand. "I'm learning things."

That made me smile at him. "Good, me, too, now let's see if I can put practice to purpose."

"Better check on Nathaniel first," J.J. said.

I looked up at my bound sweetie. His face was nearly slack with concentration, eyes focused to the side, staring at nothing. He did that sometimes when we had sex; he said it was his way of concentrating on not going.

"He's fine," I said.

"You sure?" she asked.

Nathaniel made a thumbs-up gesture.

"He's good."

J.J. moved over so we could trade places. There was always a moment before I went down on Jade where I hesitated and sort of looked at her body and thought, so many little parts, and not sure what to do with them. Men made more sense to me and were a lot easier to play with: bigger parts, less guesswork about where you should be licking and sucking.

People joke about women tasting like fish, but Jade always tasted more like meat, red meat. I'd asked Nathaniel and he'd confirmed that I did, too, but he'd also said that some women did taste like fish. If you were willing to ask the questions you could learn all sorts of things.

I teased my tongue along the edge of her, between the tiny folds of skin. She shuddered for me, and I realized that because J.J. had already brought her twice I had a head start on the next round, but that was okay, I needed the head start. I was so damn good at oral sex on men that it had sort of hurt my pride to be less spectacular with women. It had been one of the things that had made me willing to ask the questions. I would get better, damn it.

I licked on the other side of her, mirroring what I'd done, and she shuddered again—nifty! I started licking from side to side, not directly over the center of her, but going lower, so that I didn't lick over her clitoris, but below it. That would have driven me nuts, because

I liked more direct contact, but Jade's body began to shiver as I licked back and forth. Her hands convulsed on the pillow, and her breath got faster. I licked higher over her clit as I went from side to side, and her breathing sped even more, so that she started making little almost-sounds as she panted. I went back over her one more time and her body bucked, startling me, but I stayed on that sweet spot in the middle with quick flicks of my tongue, as fast as I could, like J.J. had showed me. It was a lot harder than it had looked, and I felt the beginnings of a charley horse in my tongue, so I switched to sucking, because nothing kills the mood like a muscle cramp at the wrong moment.

I sealed my mouth over her, drawing more and more of that small, happy bit of her body into my mouth, so that I was sucking it a lot like I'd suck a man, but totally different, it was just the only analogy I had. Her body bucked, up and down on the pillows and Nathaniel's body. Jade slid off the pillows, and only my grip on her thighs and other things kept her from sliding off the other side of Nathaniel.

He cried out, wordless, and I thought for a second he'd gone, too, but if he had it was trapped under Jade's body where I couldn't see the mess we'd made of the red silk. I let the thought go and kept paying attention to Jade's body, because once the orgasm started a woman could just keep going sometimes; nothing irritated me more than a man getting me to the orgasm and stopping before every last drop of pleasure was wrung from it. Until I tapped out, I didn't want someone to stop on me, so I tried to offer Jade the same, but my grip on her thighs was an awkward hold to support an entire body while she writhed and bucked. I wasn't sure I could keep sucking and change my hold, or keep doing it and not have her slide away from me on the other side of Nathaniel's body. It was one of those real-world sex problems that no one ever thinks about when you plan the group sex.

Jason was suddenly on the bed, moving with that blur of speed the wereanimals were capable of, so that he caught Jade and moved her back onto the pillows. I was able to ease my death grip on Jade's thighs and just concentrate on giving her as much orgasm as possible for as long as I could. It was the best one I'd ever managed to give her, and I wanted to make it last.

"God, you move so fast," J.J. said, "I can't wait to see what a choreographer could do with that kind of speed."

I couldn't see Jason's face without moving, and I wasn't going to do that, so I gave myself over to the woman at my mouth, under my hands. Her whole body started to shake continuously, and then a cry tore from her mouth. A cry of pleasure and release, and she collapsed boneless and motionless except for small twitches in one hand. If Jason hadn't been there to catch her she would have slipped off the pillows again, but this time he had to hold her in place as if she were unconscious from the pleasure.

J.J. tapped my shoulder. "Enough, she's done," and she laughed.

I moved back from Jade's body, my hands still on her thighs. I looked up to find Jason grinning down at me. I smiled back at him. He was cradling Jade in his arms in a way that she'd never allowed before,

though she honestly might not know who was holding her right now.

J.J. gave me a one-armed hug. "That was awesome! You learn fast."

"Being able to see and ask questions made a big
difference." I started to let go of Jade's thighs, but
looked up at Jason to make sure he wasn't depending
on my hold.

"I've got her," he said.

I put a soft kiss on her inner thigh that made her
twitch a little harder. When I rose up on my knees I
could see her eyelids fluttering, not opening, but
almost twitching like her hand. She was well and
truly gone to her happy place. Yay, fucking, yay!

Domino said, "If I hold Jade, that frees Jason up
to be with someone else."

I looked at J.J. "He's asking if you're all right
with it."

"Sure," she said.

He smiled and crawled across the bed and
Nathaniel's legs to take Jade from Jason.

"Please," Nathaniel said, voice tight, almost hoarse, though he hadn't screamed a single time.

I moved up to look into his face. His eyes were almost frantic. "Please, what?" I asked, smiling and stroking the side of his hair.

"Touch me," he whispered.

"Touch you how?"

"Hand, mouth, pussy, don't care."

Domino said, "Are you saying when I move Jade, that . . . that you didn't go?"

"Not yet," Nathaniel said, in that strangely hoarse voice.

"Wow, just wow, no wonder Anita kept you." He lifted Jade up, and Nathaniel was still long, straight, and so hard with need that he twitched involuntarily without anything touching him at all.

"I'll second that, wow," J.J. said.

"I'll third it," Jason said, and grinned. "I have good stamina, but Nathaniel puts me to shame when he wants to hold out."

J.J. looked at Jason with wide eyes, and then back

to Nathaniel, still tied and eager. "Well, um, that's . . . impressive."

Jason laughed.

Domino cuddled Jade to his chest. She was aware enough to curl in against him. Her eyes were open now, blinking heavy-lidded, and almost sleepy.

I stroked fingertips down that nearly vibrating hardness, the lightest of touches. Nathaniel cried out, body straining against the ropes.

"He won't last much longer," J.J. said.

"Don't underestimate him," I said.

She gave me a look. "Really?"

I nodded. "Really."

She gave Nathaniel a speculative look.

"It's okay," Jason said, "he inspires me to be a better man."

She frowned, clearly puzzled at Jason.

I said, "He means that when he and Nathaniel are having sex with me, he lasts longer out of competition."

She turned back to me, eyes wide, and the beginnings of a smile quirking her lips. Her chin glinted dully in the light. We both needed to clean our faces, but first, I planned to get messier. No reason to clean up before I'd finished getting all dirty.

I started bending over Nathaniel's body. His voice came almost strangled. "Oh, God, no, if you do that I'm not sure I'll last."

"Then don't last," I said.

"I want inside you."

"You said hand, mouth, or pussy, you didn't care which." I smiled at him, and he would probably have called it my "I'm going to make you sorry for that" smile when I was topping him in the bedroom/dungeon.

"Please," he said.

"Please, what?" I said, and trailed my fingertips oh-so-lightly over him again.

He cried out again. "Intercourse, sex, please!"

I kissed him, gently, where I'd just touched, and his spine bowed as if there were an invisible rope attached to the center of his body dragging him ceilingward.

His eyes had bled to leopard blue-gray when he

looked back at me. His face was as frantic as I'd ever seen it during sex. He was usually so controlled, it was interesting to see him like this; I liked it, or maybe it was just different and I wanted to try the limits of it.

I bent back over him, intending to lick the length of him and then stop and do what he wanted, probably, most likely, but he did something he'd never done with just me.

"Hopscotch," he said.

I raised up and looked at him. "You safeworded?"

"Yes," he said, in a hoarse voice that held an edge of growl to it.

"I've never heard you safeword," Jason said.

"I've only seen Asher make him safeword," I said.

"Sometimes it's not about pain, Anita. I want you, now, like this," he said, his voice deeper with the edge of the leopard that filled his eyes. He had utter control during sex, during bondage, and with his beast; if he didn't he couldn't have stripped on stage and shifted to his animal form in front of a crowd of customers—read *potential victims*.

I stared at one of the loves of my life; something about the scene we'd just done had hit some major switch for him. I'd ask him later, but for right now, I'd respect his general safeword and do what he asked.

"Jade wants some privacy," Domino said. He moved off the bed with her still curled small in his arms. I could see him tight and ready inside the red silk, but if they were leaving the room, it wasn't my problem. They were lovers, just not usually without me in the room for Jade's comfort. They'd work it out.

"Okay," I said.

"Have fun," J.J. said.

Domino smiled. "She already has, thank you."

"My pleasure," she said, and grinned.

His smile turned to a grin.

Jade murmured something to him, and whatever she'd said made him turn for the door like he had a purpose. I hoped she'd agreed to have sex with just him, but either way, not my issue. I had other fish to fry, or maybe sausage, something like that.

I looked down at Nathaniel. His eyes had bled back to their usual extraordinary lavender, but his face was still almost frantic with need. Later I'd ask him what about all of it had flipped his switch so hard, but right now I'd see just how long and how hard I could flip that switch.

11

NATHANIEL WAS ONE of those men who was longer when he was at his most excited. He could gain two inches in length between "normal" erection and this, but he was also vibratingly hard, like wrapping my hand around rock wrapped in warm, velvet skin.

I was careful as I used my hand to slide him inside me, not just because with the extra length he would be deeper inside me, but because he'd told me when he got this hard that sometimes the sensations were almost too much, so that the pleasure of being touched bordered on a type of pain, and not one he enjoyed.

I'd had sex with Nathaniel more times than I could count, but he always felt different when he was this hard, almost like making love to someone different, no matter how much my eyes saw the familiar hair, the eyes, that face, the body all achingly familiar to me, and yet as I slipped him inside me it was like my eyes and my body were telling me two different things, so familiar and not.

I shuddered as he slid inside me, and my voice shook as I said, "God, you're so hard."

He nodded and closed his eyes, his breath coming out in a shuddering line that trembled down his body and into mine, as if his whole body had shaken itself. That small movement made me close my eyes and have to fight to find my focus. I was on top, he was tied up, I was in charge; it meant I had to hold my shit together and not get completely lost in the sensations.

I kept my eyes closed and started rocking my body slowly, getting the feel of him inside me this hard. I added a hip roll, like the real version of what belly dancing promises, that deep abdominal roll, with me gripping and releasing as I rode him.

He began to move his body with mine, so that he thrust up as I squeezed down, and we began that barely moving dance, rising and falling for each other, until I made a small sound for him.

I opened my eyes and found him staring up at me. His eyes held that intensity that only shows during sex, and sometimes violence. I think because both strip us down to the bare essentials, so that we can't hide ourselves anymore, not from the person we're with, or even from ourselves. When the sex is good enough, intimate enough, there is nothing like it. I was still Christian, but I understood in moments like this why so many other faiths used sex as a religious experience. You could bend your knees in church and lie, but face to face, naked with Nathaniel buried deep inside me, there were no lies. I loved him, well and truly, and wanted nothing more in that moment than to be as close with him as I possibly could. I bent over him, changing the rhythm of my hips so I could continue to move for him, and he continued to thrust, but eventually I was bent over his body so that we were touching from groin to chest and I was staring into his eyes from inches away. I had to change the rhythm from that invisible dance of muscles and deep body to thrusting my body over him, so that more of him came out of my body, and I shoved my body down the length of him. He thrust his hips up to meet my body, so that it became more intense as we both found a matching rhythm, and I pressed my mouth to his, so that we could kiss while we made love.

His tongue thrust into my mouth so that the kiss mimicked what our bodies were doing, all of us inside each other, over and over, again, until I had to tear my mouth from his and scream my pleasure. It made me fight my body to keep the rhythm going, because I knew there were bigger orgasms waiting if we could just both hold on for a few . . . more . . . thrusts.

J.J. crawled near the head of the bed. She was watching us with something close to the intensity on

Nathaniel's face; in that moment I knew she wasn't kidding about voyeurism being one of her major kinks. Nathaniel noticed her, too, and we had a moment of looking at each other. It was a moment where one of us could have wanted more privacy, or less.

"I like an audience," he said.

"I know you do," I said, and smiled at him, and I kissed him again, so we could do that dance of eager mouths and bodies.

He pulled back enough to say, "Fuck me, Anita, please, fuck me."

I smiled and sat up straighter, so that I was riding just his hips. He started thrusting harder, deeper, using the extra flexibility he had in his hips to force himself deeper than most men could get with the woman on top. The extra length meant he hit deeper than normal, and I had a moment where it made me close my eyes and stop moving, frozen on top of him, letting his body do all the work. I started moving back and forth this time so that he stayed buried as deep inside me as he and I could manage. My rhythm grew faster, almost frantic, and he stopped moving, letting me move over him, as I'd let him control before, but from one moment to the next the orgasm washed over me, through me, tearing screams from my mouth as fast as I could draw breath. I gave myself over to the frantic dance of my body over him, so that one orgasm spilled into the next, until I couldn't tell where one ended and the other began, so it was a long spill of pleasure.

Nathaniel cried out, his body spasming, arms and legs straining, pulling at the ropes that held him down. The muscles in his arms and chest swelled as his body fought against the ropes, and the orgasm spilled his head back, bowing his back, so that his body half rose off the bed as far as the ropes and my body would allow.

He fell back against the bed, and I collapsed on top of him, feeling the frantic beats of our hearts in my chest. It was like I was lying on top of water that held a drumbeat of his heart, the pulse of his body, and between one beat and the next I fell through. The shields that kept us apart from each other vanished, and suddenly I felt my wrists and ankles bound with rope, hair spilling across my face, but it was a rougher texture than Nathaniel's hair, and curly feels different against your face than straight. I was feeling my hair flung across his face. I felt "my" body inside hers, growing soft, that afterglow of release helping everything be loose and melting, as if some tension that was always there were gone, and I could finally relax deeply and completely.

I don't know what Nathaniel felt from me in those few moments of intermingling, but I raised my head enough to feel the curly hair brush and then move from my hair, as I looked both up at my own face and down at his at the same time, so it was like being in two places at once, and then I was back inside myself, and Nathaniel blinked up at me. I wondered if I looked as startled as he did. I came back with his feelings and it was just an amazingly happy contentment, and I knew he'd gotten the same from me. I'd been told by Jean-Claude that my thoughts after sex were—not. It was one of the few times my thoughts quieted, calmed; it was the closest I got to meditating. No wonder I liked sex.

We stared at each other. "Wow," I whispered.

He smiled. "Always," he whispered back.

I smiled back. "Always."

It was one of those magical romantic moments, but we weren't alone in the room, and the other couple hadn't had their romantic moment yet. J.J. said, "Jason, come here." She was holding her arms out to him.

He crawled toward her over the bed and put that extra sway into the movement, so he seemed to have more muscles and vertebrae than a human could possibly have.

"Untie me," Nathaniel said, "want to hold you."

"I would if my lower body worked right now."

He smiled, very happy with himself at a job well done.

Jason changed the direction of his crawl and went back to the ropes around Nathaniel's right ankle. "Get his wrists," he said.

"I kind of liked the idea of him still tied up while we fucked," she said.

Jason hesitated in the midst of untying Nathaniel,

and then laughed. "You can't stay tied up forever without muscle cramps, or just getting cold."

"Oh, okay, that makes sense," she said.

"You're thinking something," Jason said, and I knew he wasn't talking to either Nathaniel or me.

"Honestly?" she said.

"Yes," he said.

I turned my head enough on Nathaniel's chest to be able to watch them. I could only see J.J.'s face and the back of Jason's body. Whatever he saw in her expression, it was lost to me; I didn't know her well enough to interpret it.

"What?" Nathaniel whispered.

I whispered back, "Not sure."

"I'm sorry the group sex is over. I had forgotten how much I fucking love to just watch."

"Would you rather watch than have sex?" he asked.

"I'm so hot from seeing it all, and what I have done, it's been amazing, and I want, need, to have sex."

"Me, too," Jason said, "but . . ." and he left the sentence unfinished so she could finish it.

"But," she said with a little smile, "I'm sorry that Anita and Nathaniel are done."

Nathaniel turned his head sort of up and backward to see her. "We don't have to be done."

"What do you mean?" she asked.

"He's multiorgasmic," Jason said, and there was no trace of envy, or negative anything, it was just a fact.

Her eyes went a little wide. "Really?"

"Really," Jason said.

"After everything you and Anita just did, and you could go again, this soon?" J.J. said.

"Untie me and let me hold Anita for a few minutes, and yes."

She gave him a speculative look and turned to me. "Really?"

"Yes," I said.

"Impressive, especially for a guy," she said.

"He is impressive," I said, and smiled, "and the two of them together are an awesome combination."

Jason turned to flash me a grin; Nathaniel bent at the neck, so I moved into the kiss he offered.

"I'd like to watch the three of you together one more time, and then when we split into couples, I'd like to go down on Anita."

"That leaves us with nothing to do," Jason said, "and if I have to watch any more girl-on-girl action without getting some action of my own, I'm going to cry."

She laughed. "So you and Nathaniel don't"—she made a vague waffling motion with her hand—"touch each other?"

They looked at each other. "We'll touch during sex if we need to steady each other," Jason said.

"You have high-fived each other over me, when you were particularly pleased with yourselves," I said.

J.J. laughed. "Really?"

"More than once," I said, and smiled. It had been a very guy moment, and almost ruined the afterglow for me the first time. Now I understood that it was the same as other male best friends high-fiving over a football win, or anything else they were interested in; sex and dancing just happened to be the two areas

213

they had most in common. Once you gave up the idea that sex was different from any other hobby, it made perfect sense.

"Nathaniel and I are just best friends, no benefits."

"Even though Nathaniel is bisexual," she said.

"His bisexuality doesn't affect my sexuality," Jason said.

"But you've been with men."

"I've tried it, and it's just not my thing, but even if I were more heteroflexible than I am, it wouldn't make Nathaniel and me lovers."

"Why not?" she asked.

He looked back at Nathaniel. They had a long look between them, and it was Nathaniel who said, "We're best friends, and you can't be best friends if you're fucking each other. It messes up the friendship."

"Some couples are best friends," she said.

"No," Nathaniel said, "once you love each other like that, you can't be true best friends."

"Best friends are who you bitch to about your

lovers," Jason said. "Can't do that if your best friend is your lover. It gets in the way."

She looked from one to the other of them. "So you two have never . . ."

"No," Nathaniel said.

"Nope," Jason said.

"I've never been around two men this comfortable with each other about sex and not have them be ex-lovers . . . I take it back, I've never been around two men this sexually comfortable around each other, even if they were ex-lovers."

"If we'd been lovers we probably wouldn't be this comfortable," Nathaniel said.

She nodded, and again I could see her thinking, just not quite what she was thinking about. I was pretty sure it was something sexual and/or relationship based, but that was my only guess.

"I'd like to have some sexual contact with Anita, oral if she'll agree, but I guess it's not fair to make you keep watching, sweetums," she said, smiling at Jason.

"I like to watch, more than Jason does," Nathaniel said.

"I'd love to look up the line of Anita's body while Jason mouth-fucked her." She closed her eyes, her body spasming with the thought that she said next: "Watching his ass go up and down, his dick going in and out of her mouth while I ate her out would be incredible."

"Agreed," Nathaniel said.

"Mouth-fucking is something very specific," I said, "and not always my favorite thing unless I let the *ardeur* out of the box, and I don't think that would be a good idea for the four of us."

"But you are great at deep-throating," J.J. said.

"That's different from mouth-fucking," I said.

She looked puzzled.

"You really haven't been with that many men, have you?"

"Not in a decade, and honestly, high school boys just didn't interest me that much, except for Jason."

"I'm not saying no to vigorous oral sex from Jason, but unless I'm in the right mood, mouth-fucking is sort of an endurance sport, and it might distract me enough that I will take a long time to go from oral myself."

"I'm not sure I understand the difference between deep-throating and mouth-fucking, and maybe you can demonstrate sometime, but anything that makes you not go from me going down on you is a no. I want you and me to enjoy it."

"I think I'll be enjoying myself, too," Jason said with a grin.

"Okay, Anita is busy at both ends, and Jason and I don't have sex together, so we're out of places for me to go," Nathaniel said.

She looked down, and I realized she was blushing. "Not completely out of places."

"No hinting, honeybunch," Jason said, "we have to be very clear on this. Are you saying that Nathaniel could have actual sex with you?"

She nodded.

"Gotta say it out loud, J.J., no misunderstandings."

"If everyone is okay with it, I'd like to try"—she

blushed harder, and then went pale—"having inter-course with Nathaniel."

Jason grinned. "I'm okay with it."

"Really?" she asked, looking up at him.

He nodded. "Really."

"So we're going to daisy-chain us all," I said.

"Maybe, or maybe we'll just break into couples again," J.J. said.

"But you with Nathaniel and me with Jason," I said.

She nodded, not looking at us, and then finally darted a glance at me. I don't know what she expected to see, but whatever she saw seemed to reassure her, because she said, "Yes, if that's okay with you?"

I smiled. "It's okay with me."

"Really?"

"Really," I said.

She looked at Nathaniel. "Are you okay with it?"

Nathaniel turned his face so she couldn't see his expression, but I got to watch him fight for a more neutral look before he turned his head back so he could see her. "Yes, very yes. Someone untie me."

"Just say it," Jason said, smiling.

"What?" J.J. asked.

"Nathaniel, just say, 'not only yes, but hell yes'!"

Nathaniel grinned and finally said with a laugh, "What you said. Now someone please untie me so we can do this."

We untied him.

12

I LAY DOWN propped on pillows, so my head was already raised to look down the line of my body, and another pillow under my ass, so that J.J. didn't get a crick in her neck. She lay down, her hands petting along my thighs and looking down at my body. "God, you're beautiful," she said, and I realized she wasn't looking at my face, or breasts, and I didn't think anyone had ever complimented that part of me in quite that way. I wasn't sure what to say, so I settled for, "Thank you."

She looked up, letting her gaze go slowly up the

line of my body, lingering on my breasts and settling on my face, meeting my eyes. The expression on her face was eager, serious, almost hungry in its heat.

"It's been a while since you got to be with someone besides your girlfriend, isn't it?"

"Yes," she said, and lowered her face to kiss the side of my hip, as she kept that intent eye contact.

"I don't think monogamy is your gig," I said, and my breath sped a little as she kissed a little more to the middle of my, um, hip.

"No," she said, and laid another soft kiss over the mound of me, and then she licked just around the edge of me. It made me catch my breath. "Oh, you're going to be fun," she said.

"Yes, yes she is," Jason said. It made us both look at him and Nathaniel on the side of the bed watching us. Jason didn't look sexual, he looked happy, content, just comfortable and happy. Nathaniel's face held more heat.

J.J. plunged her tongue lower, and it made me look at her, eyes wide. She gave me that grin that reminded me so much of Jason and then settled her mouth between my legs and began to explore. That was the only word I had for it; she ran her tongue along each fold and watched me react.

"You're seeing what works, aren't you?" I asked, a little breathless.

She rose up enough to say, "Yes, I want to see what your body reacts to, before the men join us, so I can be sure it's my tongue that's making your body jump and not something they've done."

"Sounds reasonable," I said.

She grinned again, half her smile hidden by my body. "Reasonable, I don't want reasonable."

"What do you want?" I asked.

"You screaming your orgasm for me."

I laughed, sort of startled. "Confident, aren't you?"

"Yep," she said, and put her mouth where her brag was; of course, if you're really that good, it's not bragging, it's just fact.

J.J. was good. She'd signaled the men in when she said, "I know where most of the buttons and switches are now; come help make her eyes roll back into her head."

I might have protested the wording, but she did something with her tongue that totally distracted me. Jason's face was above me, smiling. He kissed me, gently, and whispered, "Thank you."

I started to say, "My pleasure," but J.J. did something that made me cry out and try to look down at her at the same time. Jason laughed, and when I was lying back on the pillows again without spasming, he got on his knees with one leg on either side of my chest. He was nude, his shorts lost while my attention had been on J.J. I looked up the line of his body. He was already partially erect, but I didn't reach for that. I cupped the warm looseness of his balls, rolling them gently in one hand. He closed his eyes for me, and then J.J. made my whole body spasm and I had to let go of him very suddenly. My hand could safely spasm on the shaft of him, but the rest was too delicate for what my body was doing.

I said, "Oh, God."

Jason laughed.

I wrapped my hand around the shaft of him and squeezed, just enough to stop the laughter and make him shudder above me. J.J. stopped licking and started sucking, and my body spasmed for her, my hand clinching and shaking around Jason's body. He gave a soft cry, and when he looked down at me again his eyes were wild, eager.

J.J. had apparently played with all the buttons and switches she wanted, and was goal oriented on one switch in particular. She wrapped her mouth around me and licked with her tongue at the same time that she was sucking. Even as I felt the warmth begin to grow between my legs, I filed away what I was feeling to ask her how she was doing it and to see if I could duplicate it, but that was later; right now . . . I angled Jason downward and slid my mouth over him. I wanted him inside me when I came.

I sucked him, using my hand to guide him and avoid my teeth; nothing was a deal killer like an accidental tooth nick. I opened my mouth wider and moved lower on the pillows as J.J. brought me closer and closer to the edge. I slid my hands between Jason's thighs to touch his ass and press him closer to me, using my hands to start him moving in and out of my mouth. He didn't need much encouragement to start sliding himself in and out of my mouth, slowly at first, and then as I raised my mouth eagerly, he started moving faster, putting more hip movement into it, and into me. J.J. was sucking and licking harder, faster, and I wanted Jason's body to do the same to my mouth; it just seemed to work, and drive the pleasure higher to have both of them working together, so that I angled my mouth and throat eagerly, wanting him to go as far down as he could from that angle. Jason was long enough to make it enjoyable without making me feel like I was choking. It was an angle I wouldn't have tried with all the men in my life, but right that moment it worked, it totally and completely worked. My hands found the pillows and clutched at them as I let Jason move his hips as much as he wanted, and J.J. sucked hard and harder, the tip of her tongue still licking, and the building warmth crashed up and out and suddenly I was screaming my orgasm around Jason's body, until he drove himself deep enough that I couldn't scream. Sometimes that would have been too much, but tonight the feel of him down my throat, forcing my mouth wide with his body buried as tight as he could get it, was perfect for me to spasm and shiver while wave after wave of pleasure crashed over me. J.J. kept sucking, licking, so that I wasn't sure if it was all one orgasm or a series of them, one spilling into the other.

Jason drew himself out of my mouth before I was done, so I got to scream again. I heard him say, "If I don't stop, I'm going to go."

I managed to gasp, "Go . . . breasts!" I meant he could go in my mouth until he was almost ready to go, and then go on my breasts, and he seemed to understand me, because he slid himself back into my mouth and started fucking my mouth in earnest. It was almost too much, almost, and then J.J. hesitated in her sucking, and then she started sucking harder than before, so that I screamed when Jason's body let me, but in between I sank into the feel of his body slipping in and out of my mouth, down my throat, and J.J.'s mouth sucking me as if she meant to find the sweet, gooey center of my body, and make me come until I tapped out, or passed out.

And then J.J. screamed her orgasm with her mouth buried against me, and it made me scream again, my body bucking underneath them both. Jason pulled himself out of my mouth, and then he went, hot and liquid across my breasts. I opened my eyes enough to see him kneeling above me, his hand on himself aiming where I'd asked him to go, pouring himself over my breasts, so that seeing that made me scream again, and finally J.J.'s mouth wasn't on me anymore, but she was still crying out.

I fought the eye-fluttering orgasm to look down the bed and got a glimpse of Nathaniel behind J.J., and I knew exactly what was making her cry out. I'd have liked to have a better view, but the first big orgasm aftershock caught me and made me writhe underneath Jason, screaming wordlessly, my hands digging into the pillows, because he'd asked not to be scratched up, so I dug at the pillows instead of his flesh while the orgasm rocked me, and his pleasure spilled down my breasts in a happy, sticky mess.

13

THE FOUR OF us managed to crawl, fall, and collapse into a big pile. J.J. had collapsed with her upper body across my thighs and hips, Nathaniel curled around her, his hair tangled over them and my legs. Jason managed to grab the wet wipes on the bedside table so he could clean me up enough to not completely trash the sheets. As he cleaned up my breasts, he said, "I made the mess, it's the least I can do."

I gave him a thumbs-up, because I still couldn't talk or move. Good that he was mobile, good for him. But once he had me mopped up, he curled against my side, one arm across my stomach, his head resting against my shoulder.

J.J. found her voice first, though she was a little hoarse from screaming. "You both should come on one of Jason's visits to New York. We could have so much fun."

"How would you introduce Anita and Nathaniel to Freda?" Jason asked.

She rubbed her face against my thigh and said, "Anita as our lover, and Nathaniel as mine, and your best friend."

"Freda would go apeshit," Jason said, snuggling in against me a little more.

"She would," J.J. said.

I looked down at her blond hair, which was all I could see of her face. "Are you trying to use us as an excuse for the big fight?" I asked.

"Maybe," she said, and rolled her head enough to look up at me.

"Just break up with her," Nathaniel said, and he moved his face enough so I had a glimpse of his eyes through his hair.

"We share an apartment; do you know how hard it is to get a nice place at a reasonable rent in New York?"

"Are you saying that you'll try to make her move out in a huff, so you don't have to move?" I asked.

"It's a thought," she said.

I laughed. "That is cold, J.J."

"Mercenary, even," Jason said, reaching his arm down enough to stroke her hair.

"You've never tried to get an apartment in the city," she said.

"It can't be that bad," I said.

She gave me a look out of her blue eyes that was scathing and totally didn't match the warm, nefarious puppy pile we were in.

"Okay, maybe it is that bad," I said.

"Sorry to leave the cuddling, but I've got to get the condom off," Nathaniel said. He kissed J.J. on the cheek, which made her smile, and extracted himself from her and my legs. He crawled up and kissed me on the mouth, softly, thoroughly, and drew back with both of us smiling. The smile changed to something less tender and more boy as he looked at Jason. He held out his fist, and Jason fist-bumped him, grinning.

"Fist bump, really," J.J. said.

"We could high-five," Jason said.

"Shaking hands, maybe," Nathaniel suggested.

I laughed. "Go clean up, before the condom glues itself to you."

He started to crawl off the bed, and then said, "Damn, I got stuff in my hair. I'm going to have to wash it."

"That'll take forever," I said.

"Not if I don't blow-dry it, and just braid it wet."

"Okay, but then come back and cuddle," I said.

"I think we're all going to need to clean up," Nathaniel said as he got off the bed.

"Eventually," J.J. said, and crawled up so that she was on the other side of me. She lay down, propping herself up on her elbow. She touched her fingertip to my skin where Jason had missed a cleanup spot. "It was so fucking hot to watch Jason go all over you like that."

Jason started tracing the edges where his pleasure was just beginning to dry on my skin. "Wet wipes just don't clean this up, do they?"

"I'll hurry," Nathaniel said, and went for the bathroom.

J.J. looked very serious as she said, "You know, Anita, you don't have a problem with Jade being a girl, you have a problem with Jade."

I'd thought similar things in the last few hours, but I wanted to hear J.J.'s reasoning, not mine. "What do you mean?"

"She doesn't match up with you."

"I prefer women who are smaller than me, or at least not much bigger, and that's hard to find."

"But you like a woman who responds with fire, not hesitation. It seemed like every time we built up speed in the bed, Jade would do something to slow or stop the enthusiasm; that would be hard on a hard-core lesbian, let alone for your first female lover."

"Thanks for that," I said, and smiled, and then the smile vanished, "but I can't punish her for the issues her master gave her; that would be like punishing her for being a victim."

"But Anita, you don't have to have sex with someone if you don't want to, not even out of guilt."

"I'm drawn to her," I said.

"Through the metaphysical ties, I get that, but you find her a burden, not a pleasure, and that's not about her being a woman, that's about you and her not being compatible."

"How can I just kick her out of my bed? I'm the first kindness she's had in centuries."

"So it's pity sex," J.J. said.

I opened my mouth, closed it, and then tried to think instead of just denying it. I did feel sorry for Jade; who wouldn't?

Jason snuggled me closer. "I'm sorry, Anita."

I turned so that I was spooning against his body and could look at J.J. more. "Are you saying that my issue isn't having sex with a girl, but that Jade just doesn't match up with me in the bedroom?"

"If Jade were a boy, would you still be having sex

with her, or would you have gotten frustrated and moved on?"

I tried to think that one through and finally said, "I don't know."

"I do," Jason said.

J.J. looked at him, and he put his arm tighter around me, as if afraid I'd move away.

"And?" I asked, and even to me it sounded grumpy.

"Don't sound so hostile, Anita."

I think I frowned harder. "Just talk to me, Jason."

He moved his face enough so I could see him smile at me. "I've seen you kick men out of your bed that were great lovers, men you enjoyed having sex with, because some other part of their personality didn't match up with yours. I've never seen you be this patient or try this hard with any of the guys. I didn't realize how hard you've been working with Jade until today. I'm sorry that I thought it was just a sort of homophobia."

"I thought it was, too," I said.

"You'll never like women as much as you like men," J.J. said. "You like dick too much."

I half laughed. "J.J."

"It's so cute that you blush like that, but you don't need to be embarrassed that you like dick better than pussy. I love Jason, and Nathaniel is amazing, but I'll always love the girl parts better than the boy ones, and you'll always be the opposite; no harm in that."

I grinned at her and thought how perfect she was for Jason. I was so glad they'd found each other.

"You need to break up with Jade," she said.

The grin faded. "I'm all she's got."

"You're all she's got because you haven't made her find anyone else," Jason said.

"I don't know if she can take any more rejection."

Jason turned me in his arms, so I was looking up into his sincere and strangely serious eyes. "Are you really willing to spend the rest of your life trying to date someone you not only don't love, but that you actually don't enjoy having sex with? Come on, Anita, everyone else that you've passed over for regular lovers has found other people to date, or at least fuck."

"I feel guilty about them, too," I said.

"I know you do," he said, eyes still serious, but with a gentle smile to soften the edge of it.

"But why does she feel guilty?" J.J. asked.

"What do you mean?" I asked.

"Why do you feel guilty that you can't be in love with all of them, or fuck all of them? Why does that make you feel guilty?"

"They're tied to me metaphysically, some of them forever. They didn't ask to be tied to me, and I don't love them. I mean this really is until death do us part, and I don't love them."

"But you're tied to them until death do you part, too, trapped with a whole bunch of people you don't love. I'm not even sure you like all of them."

"I don't dislike any of them," I said.

She smiled and patted my arm. "It's okay, Anita, it's okay that you don't like everyone the *ardeur* has found for you."

"Before I had so much control of the *ardeur* it

could make the men, lovers, that it found for me perfect matches with me in so many ways; we think that's what happened with Micah and Nathaniel."

"Or maybe you would have loved them anyway, Anita," she said.

I shrugged. "We'll never know now, will we?"

"So you feel guilty because you had enough control to not fall in love with all of them?" she asked.

"Wait," Jason said. "Damian and Nathaniel got tied to you at the same time and you didn't fall head over heels with Damian, so just saying it's all about control level on the *ardeur* isn't true."

I stared up at him; he was right. "Why didn't I love Damian as much as Nathaniel then?"

"You were attracted to Nathaniel for a while, before the *ardeur* made him your leopard to call. You were never that drawn to Damian," Jason said.

"Damian is beautiful and great, and . . ."

"You don't have to defend him to us," Jason said.

"You don't like to reject anyone, do you?" J.J. said.

"It's not that exactly, it's more I like to include

people, not exclude them, sort of; I don't like the idea that anyone is lonely, or sad, that I'm responsible for."

"You're not responsible for all these people, Anita," J.J. said.

"Yeah, actually, I am."

Jason reached across me to rub his hand down her arm. "Actually, she sort of is."

"Explain that to me again."

I looked at Jason; he looked at me. He shook his head. "No, there is too much, I will sum up."

She laughed. "All right, give me the short version."

"Once vampires get organized, or powerful enough in any given area, they are at the top of the food chain. They see lycanthropes as less powerful, and a master vampire's metaphysical abilities usually make that true. Jean-Claude is the first-ever vampire king of America, and that makes him the leader of all the metaphysical Americans, and Anita is his queen, so in effect she is part of the leadership of all of us, and that means she is responsible for us, all of us, in a way."

"What he said."

"So, you're the queen to Jean-Claude's king, I get that, but he doesn't feel as responsible for everyone's happiness as you do. He just makes sure they have a roof over their head, food, the basics; no leader is responsible for the emotional well-being of all the people that work for him. You can't be, it's not your job."

"I've tied them to me, they can't get away, and then I reject them? It's just . . . mean."

"But you're just as trapped, Anita, and if you don't work this issue, whatever it is, that makes you feel guilty and overly responsible to them all, you're going to end up truly trapped, like forever."

J.J.'s eyes were a little too direct. I looked down and found my naked body, still sticky from Jason, with him cuddled naked beside me. He and J.J. were holding hands across my bare stomach. I looked at it all, and didn't want to have this conversation, and the moment I realized I was afraid of the conversation, was being chickenshit, I had to make myself meet that clear, blue gaze.

"There, why did you look back? You aren't happy with me, you're uncomfortable, but you're going to tough it out, right?"

"No cowardice allowed," I said.

"It's not do or die, Anita, you're just over your comfort level. It's okay not to want to look at me right now."

"Not for Anita," Jason said, drawing her over me so he could kiss her, softly.

She drew back and looked at him. "What do you mean?"

Jason looked at me. "She is one of the bravest people I know, because when she's scared, or nervous, or so uncomfortable that she wants to do *anything* but what she has to do, she does it anyway. She taught me that you can only truly be brave if you're afraid, that without fear there is no bravery."

"That's . . . admirable," J.J. said.

"You're going to embarrass me talking like that, Jason," I said.

"Well, you can return the favor by bragging on how amazing I am in bed."

I smiled, then laughed. "Well, you are fabulous, but I think your ego is pretty secure in this area."

"You guys are just going to change the subject, aren't you?"

I shrugged.

Jason shrugged.

"Boys," she said, and rolled her eyes.

"Hey, last I checked I'm a girl."

She grinned, eyes shining with that mischievous light that made me think so much of Jason. "Well, I have checked and yes, yes, you are a girl, most delightfully so."

I blushed again, and raised my hands as if that would hide it.

"Oh, yay, I made you blush twice!"

I glared at her, but couldn't keep the hard look going as she grinned at me, then Jason joined her, and the two of them undid me. I had to smile back.

"Damn it, you can both do that."

"Do what?" she asked.

"Make her smile when she doesn't want to," Jason said.

"We must use this power only for good, or when it's fun," she said.

I grinned and rolled my eyes at both of them.

"I hate to bring up something that won't make you smile, but I leave tomorrow and you need to settle this."

"Settle what?"

"Jade. You have the right to say no to her, Anita. If you've said no to men who are tied to you metaphysically, then why are you having so much trouble saying no to her?"

"I don't know."

"Is it because she's a girl?"

"*I don't know* is the only answer I have, J.J."

"Okay, let me ask you this: How do you feel about having to date Jade for the rest of your life?"

"Not great," I said.

"She's pushing you to actually date her, take her out, and make her more of your life. How do you feel about that?"

"I don't want to do it."

"Then don't," J.J. said.

I looked at her, opened my mouth, closed it, and then just lay there. I didn't know what to think, let alone feel.

Jason kissed my forehead, then rose up so he could study my face as he said, "Anita, it's okay, you don't have to date people you don't want to date."

"Easy for you to say, you're not the one they're always pushing at, demanding more from. You don't see how they look at me, the accusations, and the recriminations when I do pull away. They all want a piece of me, and there isn't enough of me for all of them."

"You said that a few weeks ago when I first asked you to help me explain things to J.J."

"It's still true," I said.

"Everyone has ex-lovers, Anita," J.J. said.

"You don't understand, J.J.; you can send your ex-lovers away. You move out, or they do, and you don't see them again. You get some distance and maybe you can be friends on down the road, but you need a little distance to get there. Every time I reject a lover they're still here. Not just in town but living in the Circus of the Damned; hell, Damian has an apartment over my garage at my house."

"Why in the world did you let him move in like that?" she asked.

"Because he's my vampire to call, and keeping your servants near you helps increase your power base."

"And you felt guilty about not loving him more," Jason said.

I gave him a dirty look. "Don't help me."

"Hey, it's the truth, and you know it."

"If you broke Jade free of her bonds to her old master, and freed others from theirs, could you break Damian free?"

"Every time I try to cut my ties with him and Nathaniel they start to die; Damian went crazy and attacked people. Jean-Claude almost had to put him down like a dangerous animal."

"Okay, then that would be a no," J.J. said, with wide eyes; she pulled the sheet more up over her, as if suddenly cold.

I grabbed a piece of sheet from her and pulled it

over me, too, because it was cold, or maybe the conversation was making me feel cold, who could tell.

"But what worked with everyone else was that you broke the bonds with their old master and replaced that master with you. What if you broke Damian's bonds with you and replaced yourself with another vampire?"

"He's tied to Nathaniel, too, remember? We'd have to cut Nathaniel free, too. I've never heard of anyone doing anything that metaphysically complex with these kinds of vampire marks."

"Has anyone ever tried?" J.J. asked.

"No, because if it goes wrong, you can break the sanity of your people, or kill them outright, which is a pretty damn big incentive to not mess with shit."

"Okay, okay, it was just a thought," J.J. said.

"I'm sorry, I'm not mad at you, just the situation, I think."

"But Damian has Cardinale, and they seem pretty happy together," Jason said.

"She's asked for Damian to not be on my feeding list for the *ardeur*, and I've respected that."

"But would he have found Cardinale if you had been having sex with him as often as you did with Nathaniel?" Jason asked.

"If I'd been sleeping with him and Nathaniel like that, there wouldn't have been room for Micah."

"You mean in the bed?" J.J. asked.

"Or in your life?" Jason asked.

I frowned at both of them. "You know, the two of you are enough alike that's it's a little unnerving."

"You feel double-teamed?" he asked.

"Didn't we already do that?" J.J. asked, face and voice mild.

I rolled eyes at them again. I got the idea that being around them would entail a lot of that for me. I didn't really mind.

"Now why didn't that get another blush?" she asked.

"No idea, my blushing is sort of unpredictable."

She fake-pouted at me.

Nathaniel came back into the room, his wet hair in a tight braid. He slipped under the sheets. "What did I miss?"

Jason and J.J. looked at each other. I said, "We don't have to tell him, I can just drop shields and he'll know what I know."

J.J. looked at me. "Really?"

"Really," I said.

Nathaniel said, "Can I cuddle in behind J.J., or do we need to switch things around?"

J.J. got an odd look on her face, and laughed. "I know we just had amazing sex, but I'd really rather cuddle with Jason."

"That's why I asked; sometimes sex is less intimate than holding afterward."

I wiggled over and J.J. got on the other side of me, so that she and Jason could spoon, and Nathaniel and I did the same about three feet away. Nathaniel wrapped his arm around me and pressed our bodies close. It had felt good for Jason to hold me, but this felt better; it was the difference between friends and more. "So, what did I miss?" he asked.

I shivered for him, just a little bit, and then let down my shields just enough and thought about the last few minutes. He didn't get the actual words, but he knew what I'd learned in the last few minutes, as if he'd been there the whole time. We'd all been getting better at sharing without overwhelming each other. Once I couldn't have done this without blasting him with emotions, memories, all of it, but now I could just share knowledge, and let him, or Micah, or Jean-Claude, put their own emotions and thoughts on it without me coloring it much.

Nathaniel snuggled in closer against me. "I'm so glad you were willing to be closer to me than you were to Damian." He kissed the side of my face, and then lower at the curve of my jaw, working down to my neck in soft, warm kisses.

"I saw Anita close her eyes, almost fluttery like during sex, and now you just know, that quickly?" J.J. asked.

"Yes," Nathaniel said, and made another kiss lower on my neck.

"What did I tell her about Jade?"

He rose up from kissing me to say, "That Jade isn't the girl for her, and she should dump her."

"I never said it like that."

"But that's how Anita interpreted it, and I got her version of the last few minutes."

"Wow, that's just . . . eerie, useful, but a little . . . I don't know, not creepy, but disturbing."

"Sweetums," Jason said, kissing her cheek, "that wasn't even on the scale of our version of creepy."

She turned enough in his arms to see his face. "Really?"

We all said *"Really"* in unison.

She looked around at all of us, and then smiled. "If I were the jealous type, it wouldn't just be Anita I was jealous of, it would be the way the three of you interact."

"What do you mean?" I asked.

"You guys are so tight as friends. I don't know if it's because you also have sex as a threesome, or more-some, but you are all just close."

"Why would you be jealous of friendships, or is it the sex?" I asked.

"Both, but Freda is jealous of my friends, and has pretty much cut me off from them. I understood the ex-lovers that I was friends with, but then she kept pushing until I really have only her in New York."

"You have friends in the dance company," Jason said.

"I did, before I spent two years with Freda; now they're just work friends, and I'm isolated from them." She looked so unhappy that I reached out and touched her arm.

She smiled at me.

"You know, it's not just me who's dating a woman that doesn't make me happy," I said.

She nodded. "We give the advice we need to hear sometimes; I heard it."

I turned enough to see Nathaniel's face. "Do you agree with J.J. about Jade?"

"I have some of the same issues you have with personal boundaries, so I'd say let's see if we can incorporate her into our sex life more as a group, and if that will satisfy her need for a relationship with you, then great, but if she keeps pushing you to go out to movies and plays with just her, then say no. You barely have time to actually date Micah, me, and Jean-Claude."

"You're usually the more the merrier," I said.

"Only with people who work their issues. It would be great to find a woman to add to us. It would make most of the other men incredibly happy, but Jade isn't the woman to help make us all happier."

"So even if she went to therapy and really worked hard at it, you veto her for more," I said, turning so I could watch his face.

He looked very serious, and a little sad, but underneath that his eyes held almost anger. I wasn't sure if he was angry at Jade, angry at the lost chance of another woman, or if he had to get angry to vote against her.

"She wants too much of you, Anita. You're already committed to too many people you love, and who fit into our lives better, and who make things better. We don't need someone who drags us down and just sucks energy. We need people who help lift everyone up and raise the energy level. Jade doesn't help enough, and she needs too much emotional hand holding without giving enough in return."

I cuddled Nathaniel's arms around me tighter. "So I get to stop dating Jade, or having sex with her?"

"Did you hear what you said, just now?" J.J. asked.

I looked at her. "I said I was breaking up with Jade."

"No, you said you 'get to' break up with her. That implies you don't really want to have sex with her, let alone date her."

"I guess I don't."

"Guess?" Jason said.

"I don't want to have sex with Jade anymore, and I sure as hell don't want to date just her, just the two of us, she's too hard emotionally."

"I hate to say it, but doesn't dumping her after tonight seem like punishing good behavior? She did let more men interact with her than ever before."

I didn't know whether to scream or cry, because it was a good point.

"Why should that change anything?" J.J. asked.

"It just does," I said, and sighed.

"It docsn't have to change everything you just decided," Nathaniel said.

I turned in his arms enough to see his face. "I'm listening."

"What parts of being with Jade do you enjoy?"

I thought about it, really thought about it. "I like taking care of her, watching her get braver and more certain of herself. I'm okay with sleeping with her beside me, lost in our puppy pile, as long as she doesn't get all freaky about the other people in the bed."

"Anything else?"

"Before this weekend I would have said I don't like having sex with other women, but it's not the girl parts, it's the personality conflicts." I looked down so I wasn't meeting anyone's eyes, and then said, "And I'm actually a little disappointed that I didn't get to watch Nathaniel have sex with J.J. I've never watched any of my guys with another woman before." I forced myself to look up then, so I had to see their faces.

Jason and J.J. were grinning at me, like

his-and-her mirror images. Nathaniel laughed behind me, that deep, happy guy laugh, and hugged me tighter.

"We'll make a voyeur out of you yet," J.J. said.

"Well, I wouldn't just want to watch," I said.

She gave me a look out of those innocent blue eyes that wasn't innocent at all. "Even better."

We talked it out a little bit more, deciding that I wouldn't cut Jade off from sex completely, but I wouldn't date her, or work to make the relationship more, because I didn't want more. I most definitely wanted less. She would have to deal. We also talked about possible sex for tomorrow that would make J.J. comfortable enough to have intercourse with Nathaniel so I could watch, with participation from Jason and me, too. It was nice to make a plan with another woman involved that didn't have to include a plan for what we'd do if the other woman freaked out about the sex. Once we'd talked it out, we took turns in the bathroom cleaning up, and then lay down to sleep with Jason and me in the middle and Nathaniel at my back, and J.J. at Jason's. She fit into the puppy pile just fine.

Keep reading for an excerpt
from the next Anita Blake novel
by Laurell K. Hamilton

DEAD ICE

Coming soon from Headline!

1

"SO, YOU'RE ENGAGED," Special Agent Brenda Manning said. She wore a black pants suit with a heavy belt that wrapped around her waist and held the gun at her side. She was FBI and didn't have to worry about concealed carry, so the fact that her gun flashed every time her suit jacket flared out wasn't an issue. The gun looked very stark as it reared up above her belt against the white button-up shirt.

"Yep," I said. My own gun was at three o'clock on me too, but I'd had my suit jacket tailored so that it flared out enough to hide the gun from the clients at my other job. Civilians spooked so easily some-times. I'd also started getting belt loops added to my skirts so I could wear a belt that would stand up to the weight of a gun and holster. I'd come straight from Animators Inc., where our motto was, "Where the Living Raise the Dead for a Killing." Bert, our business manager, didn't believe in hiding the fact that raising the dead was a rare talent, and you paid for talent. But lately my job as a U.S. Marshal for the Preternatural Branch had been taking more and more of my time. Like today.

The other very special agent, Mark Brent, was tall, thin, looking barely old enough to be out of college. He was bent over the portable computer they'd brought with them and set down on the room's only desk. He was dressed in a suit almost identical to Manning's, except his was brown to match his holster, but his gun was still a startling black bump against his white shirt. We were in the office of our head honcho, Lieutenant Rudolph Storr. Dolph was currently somewhere else, which left me alone with the FBI and Sergeant Zerbrowski. I wasn't sure which was more dangerous to my peace of mind, but I knew Zerbrowski would mouth off more. He was my partner and my friend, so he was entitled. I'd just met Special Agent Manning and I didn't owe her my life story.

"The article I read made the proposal sound amazing, like something out of a fairy tale," Manning said. She smoothed her shoulder-length hair back behind one ear and it stayed put, because it was straight as a board. My own curls would never have behaved that well.

I fought the urge to sigh. If you're a cop and a woman, never date a celebrity; it ruins your reputation for being a hardass. I was a U.S. Marshal, but ever since we'd gone public with our engagement, I'd become *Jean-Claude's fiancé*, not Marshal Blake, to most of the women I met, and a lot of the men. I'd really had hopes that the FBI would be above such things in the middle of fighting crime, but apparently not.

The real problem for me was that the story we told publicly was both true and a lie. Jean-Claude had done the big gesture, but only after he'd proposed in the middle of shower sex. It had been spontaneous and wonderful and messy, and very real. I'd said yes, which had surprised him, and me. I'd figured I just wasn't the marrying kind of girl. He'd told me then that we'd need to do something to live up to his reputation, for the media and the other vampires. They expected their king/president to have a certain flair, and the real proposal had been too mundane. I hadn't understood that flair would include a horse-drawn carriage—yeah, you heard me, he actually picked me up in a freaking horse-drawn carriage. If I hadn't already said yes, and loved him to pieces, I'd have told him not only no, but hell no. Only true love had gotten me to play along with a proposal so grand that trying to imagine a wedding that topped it sort of scared me.

"Oh, yeah, Anita is all into that princess stuff, aren't you, Anita?" Zerbrowski called from the chair he was half tipping against the wall. He looked like he'd slept in his suit, complete with a stain on his crooked tie. I knew he'd left his home freshly washed and tidy, but he was like Pigpen from the Peanuts comic; dirt and mess just seemed to be attracted to him within minutes of his walking out of his house. His salt-and-pepper hair was getting more salt and less pepper, and had grown out enough to be all messy curls, which he kept running his hands through. Only his silver-framed glasses were square and gleaming clean around his brown eyes.

"Yeah, I'm all about that princess shit, Zerbrowski," I said.

Agent Manning frowned at both of us. "I'm getting the idea that I stepped in something. I was just trying to be friendly."

"No, you were wanting the princess to talk about how wonderful the prince is, and how he swept her off her feet," Zerbrowski said, "but Anita is going to disappoint you like she's disappointed the last dozen women to ask questions about the big romantic gesture."

I wanted to say it wasn't a big romantic gesture, it was a freaking epic romantic gesture and I had hated it. Jean-Claude had loved being able to finally pull out all the stops and just do what, apparently, he'd wanted to do for years while we dated—the whole princely "sweep you off your feet" shit. I liked to keep my feet firmly on the ground unless sex was involved, and you can't really have sex in a horse-drawn carriage; it scares the horses. No, we didn't try, because we were on freaking camera the whole time. Apparently, there are now engagement coordinators just like there are wedding coordinators, so of course we had a videographer. It had been all I could do to keep from scowling through all of it, so I'd smiled for the camera and so I wouldn't hurt Jean-Claude's feelings, but it's not my real smile and my eyes in a few frames have that wait-until-we're-alone-mister-we-are-so-talking-about-this look.

I decided to appeal to Manning's sisterhood of the badge, and said, "Sorry, Agent Manning, but ever since the story went live I'm getting treated more like Jean-Claude's girlfriend than a marshal, and it's really beginning to bug me."

Her face went serious. "I'm sorry, I hadn't thought

about it like that. Years of being one of the guys and building your rep, and I ask you about your engagement first thing."

"I've never seen my partner be so girl about anything as meeting you today, Marshal Blake," Brent said as he unbent from hunching over the computer. He smiled and it made him look even younger. He seemed fresh faced and less jaded than the rest of us. Ah, to be bright and shiny again, when you thought you could actually win the fight against evil.

Manning actually looked embarrassed, which isn't something you see often in FBI agents, especially not when you've just met them.

"Knock it off, Brent," she said.

He grinned at all of us. "It's just that we've worked together for two years, and I've never seen you squee over anything."

"It's the horse-drawn carriage," Zerbrowski said. "Chicks dig that kind of shit."

"Not this chick," I said, quietly under my breath.

"What did you say?" Manning asked.

"Nothing. Is the video ready, Agent Brent?" I

asked, hopeful we could actually do our jobs and leave my personal life out of it.

"Yes." Then his smile faded around the edges, and I saw the beginnings of the bright and shiny rubbing off. "Though after you see it, we may all be game to talk about carriages and pretty, pretty princesses."

It was another first, an FBI agent admitting that something bothered them. For him to admit it out loud, it had to be bad. I suddenly didn't want to see it. I didn't want to add another nightmare to the visuals I had in my head. I was a legal vampire executioner and raised zombies as my psychic talent. I had enough scary shit in my head that I so didn't need more, but I stayed in my chair. If Manning and Brent were tough enough to watch it multiple times, I could sit through it once. I couldn't let the other badges think that getting proposed to by the vampire of my dreams had made me one bit less tough. I couldn't let myself believe it either, though a part of me did. How could someone who let a man lead her into a

Cinderella carriage carry a gun and execute bad guys? It made even my head hurt, thinking about it.

Zerbrowski said what I was thinking. "I thought the feds never admitted anything bothered them."

Agent Brent shook his head, and looked tired. Lines showed around his eyes that I hadn't seen before and made me add between three and five years to my estimate of his age. "I've worked in law enforcement for six years. I'd thought I'd seen it all, until this."

I did math in my head, and realized he had to be nearly thirty, which was how old I was, but I'd used up my shininess years ago.

"I thought this was just another big, bad preternatural citizen gone wrong," I said.

"Not exactly," he said.

"I don't like mysteries, Agent Brent. I'm only here with this little information out of courtesy to the FBI, and because Captain Storr requested it."

"We appreciate that, Marshal, and we wouldn't have had you walk into this blind if we didn't feel that the fewer people who know the details, the better off we're going to be," Brent said.

"Awesome," I said, "but the foreplay is getting a little tiresome. There's no one in the room but the four of us, so what is on the video?"

"Are you always this cranky?" Manning asked.

Zerbrowski laughed out loud, and didn't even try to hold it in. "Oh, Agent Manning, this isn't even close to cranky for my partner."

"We heard that about her, and you're right, Blake. I did come in here expecting the proposal to have softened that reputation. I didn't think I had that much girl left in me, and if I'm assuming that it softened you up, then your male colleagues must be making your life . . . difficult."

It was my turn to laugh. "That's one way of putting it, but honestly it's the whole engaged-to-a-vampire thing that's making some of my fellow officers doubt whose side I'm on."

"Vampires are legal citizens now, with all the rights that entails," she said.

"Legally, yeah, but prejudice doesn't go away just because a law changes."

"You're right about that," she said. "In fact, some at the Bureau thought we shouldn't include you in this case because of your proclivity to date the preternatural."

"Proclivity, that's polite. So what made you decide to trust me?"

"You still have the highest kill count of any vampire executioner in the United States, and only Denis-Luc St. John has more rogue lycanthrope kills than you."

"He raises Troll-Hounds. They're the only breed of dog ever raised specifically to hunt supernatural prey. It makes him the king of tracking through wilderness areas after shapeshifters."

"Are you implying that the dogs make him better at the job, or that he's somehow cheating by using them?" she asked.

I shrugged. "Neither, just a statement of fact."

"Now that Anita has passed muster, and I'm

included because I'm her friend, show us some skin, agents, or stop teasing," Zerbrowski said.

"Oh, you'll see skin," Brent said, and he looked older again.

"What the hell is on the video, Agent Brent?" I asked.

"Zombie porn," Brent said, and hit the arrow in the middle of the screen.

2

"SORRY, AGENTS, BUT that's not new. It's sick, but it's not new."

Brent hit the screen and froze the dark cemetery scene in midmotion. It was shaky and dark, and there were no zombies or anyone else in sight yet. The two agents looked at me as if I'd said something bad.

"Did we pick the wrong animator?" Manning asked her partner.

"Maybe," he said.

"I've been approached for years to help people

make sex tapes with zombies. Dead celebrities bring out the creeps the most." I shivered, because the whole thought of it was just so wrong.

"My favorite of your sickos like that are the ones who want you to raise their high school crush," Zerbrowski said.

"Yeah, now that they have money and success they want one more go at the girl who rejected them in high school, or college." I shook my head.

"That's sick, as in seek-a-therapist sick," Manning said.

"Agreed, and I honestly think they don't really believe it's going to be a zombie. Somewhere in their minds they think she'll rise from the grave and he'll be able to prove he's worthy and live happily ever after."

"Wow, Anita, that's a romantic take on the sick bastards that just want to boff the girl who rejected them in high school." Zerbrowski actually looked surprised.

I shrugged, fought off a scowl, and finally said, "Yeah, yeah, one epic proposal and I go all girlie on you."

"*Boff*," Agent Brent said. "I didn't know people used that word anymore."

"You young whippersnappers just don't know a good piece of slang when you hear it," Zerbrowski said.

"Don't listen to him, he's not that old. His hair just went all salt-and-pepper early."

"It's the last couple of cases, they scared me so bad my hair went white." He delivered it without a grin, deadpan, which he never did, and if they'd known him, they would have understood he was lying, but they didn't know him.

"Hair doesn't actually do that from fear," Brent said, but not like he completely believed it.

Manning looked at me, raised an eyebrow.

I waved her back to Zerbrowski. "It's his story, not mine."

Zerbrowski grinned at me, and then at the agents. "Just trying to lighten the mood, that's part of my charm."

"It is, actually," I said, smiling back at him.

"The sergeant is here because he's your partner

when you work with the Regional Preternatural Investigation Squad. Everybody calls it the Regional Preternatural Investigation Team, but officially it's not," Manning said.

"It's the nickname," I said, "they call us RIPIT, both for the 'Rest in Peace,' and because most of the crimes are violent, things get ripped apart. Other cops and even the media have used RIPIT for so long that people want the *T* in the actual name of the squad."

"Are we letting ourselves get sidetracked on purpose?" Brent asked.

Manning nodded, and sipped her coffee. "I think we are, so back on target. Another reason we're talking to you is that you have made more official complaints to the police than any other animator about illegal or morally questionable zombie-raising requests. Once you had a badge of your own and were officially an officer, too, the complaints went down. I'm assuming that people didn't want to bring their illegal activities to a U.S. Marshal."

"You'd be surprised how many people think that

just because I raise the dead I have to be evil, with a capital *E*, but yeah, the requests for zombie one-nighters and zombie sex slaves went down once I could do my own arresting."

"Disturbance of a corpse was a misdemeanor for years," Manning said.

"That's one of the reasons there are tapes of this shit out there, because even if they were caught, it was a slap on the wrist. The money they could make from the tape, because it was a tape back when it started, was worth the risk even if they were caught," I said.

"The penalties are stiffer now, but still not the same as if a real human were involved," she said.

I shrugged. "I don't make the laws, just help enforce them."

"You have done your best to enforce the laws as written, and suggested changes in the laws based on your experience, which is one of the reasons we picked you to bring into our little problem," Manning said.

"We all know it's out there, agent, so what's the

big secret? All the other zombie porn has been either people in good makeup, with no real zombies involved, or one of the zombies that's been raised for fieldwork in California, or in other countries. The zombies in those films are little better than actual corpses."

"These are different," Manning said.

"Show us," I said, and added, "please." I added the *please* because what I really wanted to say was either *you're being all wimpy for FBI* or something more sarcastic. I'd been a little grumpy lately, even for me, so I was trying to monitor myself and only aim the grumpiness at bad guys.

Brent hit the screen again and the shaky camerawork continued to be shaky so that you could see it was a cemetery at night, but that was about it. It was like the opening to an amateur horror flick where someone had gotten a new camera for Christmas, and then it steadied. I wondered if someone new was holding the camera, or if the holder had just gotten a handle on it. The answer to that question was the difference between one bad guy and two.

There was a very abrupt jump in the film from empty cemetery to a blond woman clawing her way out of the grave. At first I thought it was an actress who had been buried in soft earth to about her armpits, but then the camera got a close-up of the eyes and I knew dead when I saw it. The zombie crawled out of the grave the way I'd seen thousands do before. It had some issues with the skirt of the dress it had been buried in, and the clinging grave dirt, which happened sometimes, and then it stumbled free, standing crooked because one high heel had apparently been left in the grave.

The body was tall, statuesque, with blond hair to her shoulders. Cleavage showed at the plunging neckline of the white dress, which meant the breasts had probably been implants. Real breast tissue wasn't going to be that perky without a woman fluffing them back into place, and the zombie didn't know enough to do that. The small spotlight or whatever was attached to the handheld camera showed us the eyes were pale gray that might have been bluer when she was alive. Blue mingled with any color from gray to green or even hazel tended to shift with a person's moods more than most eye colors. Alive, she'd probably been beautiful, but there wasn't enough home for that now. So much of a person's attractiveness is their spirit, their personality. Zombies didn't have much of that.

The next scene, if that's what you wanted to call it, was of the zombie in a standard bedroom except there were no visible windows in the room, and there was just something off about it. I wasn't sure why I didn't like the room, but I didn't. The zombie was wearing the same clothes as in the cemetery, they hadn't cleaned her up at all, so that she looked horror-movie wrong in the bedroom with its flowered bedspread and tile floor. That was part of the wrong; no one put tile in their bedroom. They did another zooming close-up of the zombie's eyes and this time they weren't empty. This time they were terrified.

"FUCK," I SAID, softly but with real feeling.

"You see it, too, then," Manning said.

"Yeah, I see it."

Zerbrowski said, "Why do the eyes look scared? Zombies don't feel fear, right?"

"Normally, no," I said.

Zerbrowski got up from his chair and moved over closer to where the rest of us were sitting. "Why do the eyes look like that, then?"

"We don't know," Manning said. "What you're about to see is impossible according to our own experts."

My skin was already cold, my stomach tight, because I was very afraid that I knew exactly what the "impossible" was going to be.

A man in one of those all-leather masks so that only his eyes and mouth showed walked into sight. The zombie's eyes followed the movement, but the rest of her stood immobile. Probably she'd been told to stand there, and until told otherwise, she had to just stand there, but they hadn't told her not to move her eyes, so she followed the man's movements like a human victim who had been tied up. She was tied up, tighter than any rope or chain could ever make her. Fuck, I did not want this little film to go where it was headed. I prayed silently, *Please, God, don't let them be able to do this to her.* God answers all prayers, but sometimes the answer is no.

The man slipped his hand inside her dress and began to fondle her breast. The camera caught the flinching in her eyes; she so didn't want him to do it, but nothing except her eyes was able to say no.

"Did they give her a sedative that keeps her immobile?" Zerbrowski asked.

"We looked into that," Manning said, "and if she'd been alive then maybe, but we know she isn't alive. Notice she never breathes. A live human being needs to breathe. She's a zombie, so she could be kept immobile just by orders from whoever raised her."

"Does she breathe in later films?" I asked.

"She talks, and you have to take air in to do that, but other than that, no."

The man was wearing a pair of silk boxers with hearts on them, like a parody of dressing up for a romantic evening, except for the mask, which didn't match the almost silly-looking shorts. Yes, I was concentrating on details that might help me find any clue to who this was or where it was happening, but I was also already trying to concentrate on the details that wouldn't haunt me as much. The silly heart shorts were almost a kindness, a break in the horror, like whoever was picking out the costumes had goofed.

I missed the heart-covered shorts when he stripped them off, because then I had to concentrate on his body, looking for birthmarks, or tattoos, or anything that made him not a generic guy in a mask. I didn't want to look at his body, didn't want to search every inch of it for identifying marks. I wanted to look away, but if the woman, because that's what the eyes meant, if the woman in the film had to endure it, then I wouldn't look away. I would not flinch and miss some visual that might lead us to these bastards. Though part of me knew that if just watching the films would lead anywhere, the FBI would have found it by now. But I watched it anyway, because most cops believe that they will see something that everyone else has missed, it's the hope that keeps us all putting on the badge and gun every morning. When that hope runs out, we find different jobs.

A man off camera told her to lie on the bed and she did it instantly even while her eyes showed just how much she didn't want to do it. The naked man in front of the camera slid her panties down those long legs that were still covered in grave dirt, the one high heel still on. Someone had painted her toenails a soft pink, as if it still mattered with closed-toe shoes and a corpse. I expected more of her clothes to come off, but the naked man just climbed on top of her with no preliminaries, except to move her dress a little out of the way.

Zerbrowski breathed out, "Jesus," behind me.

I didn't look at him, I didn't look at anybody, and none of us looked at each other, because when watching this kind of shit, no one wants eye contact. You don't want the other officers to know you're afraid, or too emotional, and if anything this awful excites you, you don't share that either. None of the other cops want to know.

The only plus was that the camera had moved

back enough to catch the sex, so we couldn't see her eyes. She just lay there like the corpse she almost was, and that was the only tiny saving grace. He ended by taking his dick out of her body and did the obligatory porn movie end to show that he'd actually gone.

The film ended there, and I felt my gut loosen a little. I'd watched it all, bully for me. Bully for us all.

"The production value goes up as the films progress," Brent said.

I turned and looked at him. "What do you mean?"

"The almost joke-worthy boxers go away, but the camerawork gets better, and they put more personal touches around the bedroom to make it look less like a set and more real," he said.

"Is it always the same guy on stage?" Zerbrowski asked.

"For most of the films, but there's a second, younger-looking guy featured in the last two," Brent said.

"How many films are there?" I asked.

"More than I want to sit through again," Manning said.

I looked at her and saw a terrible tiredness in her eyes, as if just watching the one film had aged her. She shook her head. "Play the next one, Brent; let's just get this over with."

I didn't tell her she didn't have to watch them again, I let her handle her own shit, to do anything else would have been a breach of the "guy code" that all police work revolved around. The sex of the police officer didn't change the code. I only broke it with friends, or when I couldn't help myself, like Manning had when she asked about my engagement. That seemed like a long time ago, and Brent was right: pretty, pretty princess talk was looking a whole lot better.

3

THE FILMS WERE relentless. They eventually got her out of her burial clothes. We saw the zombie naked, in lingerie inexpertly put on her, so that I was pretty sure there was no woman on their crew. By the fourth film the zombie looked more rotted, which is something that happens to zombies eventually, no matter how good they look at the beginning. Zombies rot, it's one of the things that sets them apart from ghouls, or vampires; not all corpses are created equal.

I waited for the rot to spread, but it didn't. It just

stayed with one eye filmy white, while the other was still clear and grayish-blue. Her skin had taken on a bluish tinge, and the cheeks had begun to collapse inward; the breasts were only perky because the implants held them up, but her body looked different naked now, more skeletal, but that was it. There were no other changes, the rot just stopped in midprocess, and her eyes were still full of terror. Sometimes they let her talk and she begged them not to make her do this or that, but seemed unable to disobey that male voice just off camera. I was betting it was the animator who had raised her from the grave. At first I'd thought the animator had raised her, taken his money, and fled, but now I knew he had to be nearby, because the rot had started and then stopped, and for that you needed voodoo of the blackest kind.

"Well," Zerbrowski said, "I'll give the sleazebag props for stamina, but it's a shame that abuse of a corpse isn't a capital crime."

Brent paused the images; I think any excuse at this point to take a breather sounded good to all of us. "We thought they were just changing clothes on her to make it look like time was passing, at first," Brent said. "But notice the calendar on the wall."

"It's not just there to make it look more homey?" Zerbrowski asked. He made little air quotes around "homey."

"Nobody puts a calendar in their bedroom unless it's the only space they have to live in," I said.

"Exactly," Manning said, "did you notice?"

I thought for a second. "The month changed."

"Zombies rot, always, that's the rule that Anita taught me. It can't be a month later."

She nodded. "It's not proof that much time actually passed, but we think it may be their way of showing clients that they've done something very unique."

"Her soul is back in her eyes, that wasn't unique enough?" I asked, and my voice didn't sound neutral the way I tried to sound this early in an investigation. I wasn't sure I was going to be able to pull off neutral with this case; sometimes you can't.

"You saw it," Manning said.

"We both saw it," Zerbrowski said.

"Would you have said her soul was back in her eyes, Sergeant?"

"I'm not that poetic."

Manning looked at me. "I don't think Marshal Blake was being poetic."

Zerbrowski looked from her to me. "I think I'm missing something."

"Don't feel bad," Brent said, "it took us weeks to figure it out."

"Figure out what?" he asked.

"Were you being poetic, Marshal Blake?" Manning asked.

"No."

"Enlighten us," she said, and there was something in the way she said it that I didn't like. It was just an undercurrent, but if I had to bet, I think something I'd said, or done, while we watched the films had made her suspicious of me. I wondered, if it hadn't been a male voice ordering the zombie around, if they'd have looked at me as a suspect from the beginning. I hoped not, but a lot of people still saw my psychic ability as evil. Hell, the Catholic Church had excommunicated us all unless we gave up raising the dead, because only Jesus was allowed to do that. Biblical scholars had pointed out that four of his disciples had done it, too, but the Pope, at the time, had found comparing zombie-raising pagans to the disciples of Jesus Christ less than amusing.

"Her soul, her personality, whatever you want to call it, seems to be in the body, except you can't raise a zombie from the grave if the soul is still in residence," I said.

"So how do you explain it?" she asked.

"She was just a walking corpse in the first film. Her eyes were empty, she was an it, but between that and the first sex tape that changed."

"How?" Manning asked.

"You've got witches and psychics on the payroll at the FBI now. You even have at least one animator. What'd they come up with?"

"Nothing," she said.

Brent added, "They all saw what you see, that she was in there somehow, but no one had a clue how it was accomplished."

"Do you know how it was done?" Manning asked.

I nodded. "I've seen it done once."

"Give us a name and we may have our guy," Brent said, all eager for a clue.

"It was a woman, and she's dead." I added, "I believe she's dead."

"Give us a name, we're good at finding people," Manning said.

"Dominga Salvador. She was the most powerful vaudun priestess in the midwest."

"She went missing just after she challenged you."

I raised eyebrows at Manning. "Challenged me? You mean sent killer zombies into my apartment to murder me? If that's your definition of challenge, then okay."

"Some of the local law enforcement officers thought you'd killed her in self-defense."

"The local leos didn't trust me as much before I had a badge."

"I trusted you," Zerbrowski said.

I smiled at him. "You liked me. I don't know if you trusted me."

He grinned and seemed to think about it. "I can't remember for sure, but I know that long before you got your own badge you proved anything you needed to prove to me."

"Aw, shucks, Zerbrowski, you're going to make a girl blush."

He grinned wider and offered me his fist. I bumped it gently.

"Nice distraction there, Sergeant," Manning said.

"I don't know what you mean, agent," he said.

Her lips curled down in a face that said, clearly, she knew that he knew exactly what he'd done. "It's going to take more than that to distract me."

"And that's the truth," Brent said. His partner gave him an unfriendly look and he held his hands out empty, as if to say, didn't mean any harm.

"Why do you think Dominga Salvador is dead?" Manning asked.

"Because I'm alive, and once a person like the señora wants you dead, she doesn't give up."

"How do you think she died?"

I tried to appear nonchalant and was glad that I

did a better blank-cop face than I had years ago when I'd known Dominga Salvador, because I was about to tell a very big lie to the FBI. "I have no idea." I could feel my pulse speed in my throat, if I'd been on a Polygraph, I'd have failed.

Manning studied my face like she'd memorize the number of eyelashes I had. I stayed blank and slightly smiling, and felt my eyes dead and empty as last year's New Year's resolutions. I wanted to look away from her so badly it almost hurt, but I didn't. I knew exactly how Dominga Salvador had died, because I had killed her.

Affliction

Laurell K. Hamilton

Had everyone bitten tonight caught this? The other bites had not looked like vampire bites. They'd been zombie, or human looking. Was this infection something that vampires and shapeshifters could catch? If it was, then it was something new.

Some zombies are raised. Others must be put down. Just ask me, Anita Blake, Vampire Hunter. Before now, I figured I could handle them. Before now, I had never heard of any of them causing human beings to perish in agony. But that's all changed. These creatures hunt in daylight, and are as fast and strong as vampires. If they bite you, you become just like them. And round and round it goes . . .

Where will it stop? Even I don't know.

Praise for Laurell K. Hamilton:

'Hamilton remains one of the most inventive and exciting writers in the paranormal field' Charlaine Harris

'Anita Blake is one of the most fascinating fictional heroines since Scarlett O'Hara' *Publishers Weekly*

978 0 7553 8904 9

headline

Kiss The Dead

Laurell K. Hamilton

I knew without doubt that if any more of the vampires tried to attack us I'd kill them, too, regardless of apparent age, race, sex, or religious affiliations. I was an equal-opportunity executioner; I killed everybody.

My name is Anita Blake and I am a vampire hunter and necromancer, as well as a US Marshal. So when a fifteen-year-old girl is abducted by vampires, it's up to me to find her. And when I do, I'm faced with something I've never seen before: a terrifyingly ordinary group of people – kids, grandparents, soccer moms – all recently turned and willing to die to avoid serving their vampire master. And where there's one martyr, I know there will be more . . .

But even vampires have monsters that they're afraid of. And I'm one of them . . .

Praise for Laurell K. Hamilton:

'Hamilton remains one of the most inventive and exciting writers in the paranormal field' Charlaine Harris

'Anita Blake is one of the most fascinating fictional heroines since Scarlett O'Hara' *Publishers Weekly*

978 0 7553 8900 1

headline

Hit List

Laurell K. Hamilton

We followed the fresh blood even though
every molecule in my body was screaming
for me to run. Run before dark. Run before
the Vampires come. Run.

My name is Anita Blake. The vampires call me 'The Executioner'. After a series of gruesome murders in the Pacific Northwest, the local police call in me and fellow US Marshal Edward to track down a serial killer they are convinced must be a 'monster'.

But I know that some monsters are very real. The Harlequin are a secret so dark, even to speak their name can earn you a death sentence. Now they're here, hunting weretigers and human police. And me.

The Harlequin serve the Mother of All Darkness, the first vampire. Back from the dead, she's determined to kill Edward and to possess me. And she doesn't care how many others have to die along the way.

Praise for Laurell K. Hamilton:

'Hamilton remains one of the most inventive and exciting writers in the paranormal field' Charlaine Harris

'Anita Blake is one of the most fascinating fictional heroines since Scarlett O'Hara' *Publishers Weekly*

978 0 7553 5261 6

headline

Bullet

Laurell K. Hamilton

If I had ever wanted to give in to hysterics, it was then. How do you fight something with no body to kill? How do you fight something that can possess the most powerful vampires in the world and use them like puppets?

My name is Anita Blake and I try very had to live a normal life in St Louis – as normal as possible for someone who is a legal vampire executioner and a US Marshal. But then a vampire from my past reaches out. She was supposed to be dead, but the Mother of All Darkness is the first vampire, the dark creator, and it's hard to kill a god.

She believes that the triumvirate created by master vampire Jean-Claude with me and the werewolf Richard Zeeman has enough power for her to regain a body and to emigrate to the New World. But the body she wants to possess is already taken; I'm about to learn a whole new meaning to sharing my body, one that has nothing to do with the bedroom. And if she can't succeed in taking over my body for herself, she means to see that no one else has the use of it, ever again . . .

'Hamilton remains one of the most inventive and exciting writers in the paranormal field' Charlaine Harris

978 0 7553 5258 6

headline

Flirt

Laurell K. Hamilton

I've earned my reputation, but if you really did
your research on me then you also know that
I don't raise zombies for kicks, or thrill seekers,
or tormented relatives unless they have a plan ...

I am Anita Blake, vampire hunter and necromancer,
and when I meet with Tony Bennington, who is
desperate to have me reanimate his recently deceased
wife, I feel sympathy for his loss. After all, I know
something about love, and I know everything there is
to know about loss. But I also know that what I can do
as a necromancer isn't the miracle Tony thinks he
needs. The creature that I could coerce to step out of
his late wife's grave would not be the lovely Mrs
Bennington. Not really. And not for long.

I have been relaxing just a bit with the men in my
private life. The affectionate warmth of being with
them seems to bring out something softer in me, a
sense of safety I can almost trust. They do love me;
that part is for ever and for sure. But flirting with
feeling safe is a dangerous thing ...

'Hamilton remains one of the most inventive and
exciting writers in the paranormal field' Charlaine
Harris

978 0 7553 7437 3

headline

Now you can buy any of these bestselling books
by **Laurell K. Hamilton** from your bookshop
or *direct from her publisher*.

Guilty Pleasures	£7.99
The Laughing Corpse	£7.99
Circus of the Damned	£7.99
The Lunatic Cafe	£7.99
Bloody Bones	£7.99
The Killing Dance	£7.99
Burnt Offerings	£7.99
Blue Moon	£7.99
Obsidian Butterfly	£7.99
Narcissus in Chains	£7.99
Cerulean Sins	£7.99
Incubus Dreams	£7.99
Micah and Strange Candy	£7.99
Danse Macabre	£7.99
The Harlequin	£7.99
Blood Noir	£7.99
Skin Trade	£7.99
Bullet	£7.99
Hit List	£7.99
Kiss the Dead	£7.99
Affliction	£7.99
Jason	£7.99